Reeds in my Veins

A novel

Chipiwa Mafemba

Cover Designer, Copyright © 2021, by Farai Macheka

Content editor: Chipo Musikavanhu

First Edition.

This novel is a work of fiction. Names, characters, places, and incidents either are the product of the author's imagination or are used fictitiously. Any resemblance to actual events, locales, organizations, or persons living or dead is entirely coincidental and beyond the intent of either the author or the publisher.

ISBN: 978-0-620-94685-8

DEDICATION

In The Republic of South Africa, August is a month in which women are commemorated and celebrated for their bravery, courage, determination amongst many other of their attributes. With Reeds in my Veins being published in the month of August, I would like to pass my gratitude to all the phenomenal women that have contributed in moulding my personality, character and have served as great inspiration in my journey of life. Thank you.

CONTENTS

AUTHOR'S NOTE

2019 to date, 2021, has been a dreadful phase due to the merciless pandemic COVID-19. It callously and prematurely claimed the lives of many loved ones. I would like to send my heartfelt love to all families at loss. And to those whose sun of life has set, the memories you left behind live on; you might be out of sight but not out of mind.

In the process of completing this book, I drew my inspiration from the need to stay courageous in the ongoing fight against any manner of ill-health. May we all find inspiration to live and may we conquer the war.

1 Restrained

Shewe was a man of great deference in the small village of Muromo located in Manicaland. He had partnered with the missionaries who had settled in the village, to assist with educating and raising awareness of the Christian way of life in the community. His duty came with social expectations and obligations. Shewe and his household had to lead lives that were in strict alignment with the laws of the Bible with the purpose to uphold their Christian status. Emphasis on preclusion of sex out of wedlock and a lifestyle of peace was the order of the day.

On the contrary his unmarried daughter had fallen pregnant. Vimbai and Panganai had grown up together in the 'well' coordinated community of the intimate village. The pervasive patriarchal system had clawed its nails into the schooling system that was offered. It provided for the males only and it merely equipped them for black collar jobs. Fed up with the manner of education he received, Panganai had dropped out of school and left the village in search for greener pastures in the big city, Salisbury.

Having known each other from childhood, Vimbai and Panganai had grown fond of each other and as a result they had innocently fallen in love. In the wake of attaining a job at a white owned wheat mill, he would regularly return to the village to see his family and he would fervently pay Vimbai visits of course bearing a gift from the city for her. Having shared with her his intentions to marry her, he had mentioned that it was saving for *roora*[1] that was delaying him.

The gifts and promises allowed Vimbai to optimistically dream and visualize a future with her beloved. She was certain that all she ever wanted was to be Panganai's wife and build a family with him. Most young men in the village had been absorbed into the army leaving the young girls in despair of their marriage destinies, but not Vimbai she was amongst the few lucky ones and most girls were in awe of her.

Brutal governance in Rhodesia had intensified causing the purge of frustration amongst the majority. By late 1977, the situation had worsened; the colonial regime had become more comfortable endorsing the constant oppression of the majority population. People had had enough of being peaceful such that a substantial number of young men were passionately engaging in the proceedings of war. Their aim--to regain their freedom, rightful treatment, respect, and reclaim ownership of the seized resources. These were the murmurings of a revolution brewing!

Sitting on the dusty ground of the river bank, with his back leaned against the stodgy trunk of the fig tree and his

---

[1] the practice of the African custom by which the bridegroom's family asks for the hand in marriage to the bride by offering her family a token of appreciation for raising her well. It is in the form of cattle, cash and various gifts.

gaze fixed on the melodious flow of Odzi river. He reached for Vimbai's hand. She was sitting next to him sharing the view. He muttered, "Vimbai I love you".

"*Unogaro daro iwe Panga,*[2]" responded Vimbai as she stood.

"*Ndirikurevesa mudiwa.*[3]"

"*Ndozviziva, neni ndokudawo mufunge asika*[4]...," she completed her sentence with a satirical scoff and looked at her Panganai.

"*Ndozviziva zvaurikuda kutaura. Vimbai ndirikuronga kana neniwo ndave kuda kuita samusha, ndakuunzira chuma ichi rega ndikupfekedze*[5]".

He gently took her right hand and put on her wrist a handmade band of beads and a piece of cubic-zirconia. It was beautiful against her dark pearly skin she could not stop turning it with admiration.

"*Pese paunochitarira chikucherechedze nezvechitsiidzo chedu,*[6]" he said charmingly to edify her joy.

"*Maitabasa*[7] Samanyanga."

"*Usati waenda ndine zvandikuda kukupa tichine nguva chimbomira*[8]......"

---

[2] you always say that Panganai

[3] I mean it my love

[4] I know, I love you too but...

[5] I know what you want to say. Vimbai I am making a plan, I also want us to get married, however here is a bracelet I got for you, let me help you put it on

[6] Whenever you look at it may it remind you of the promises we have made to each other

[7] Thank you

[8] Before you go there is something I would like to give you, don't be in a hurry to go we still have time

"Usandifurire iwe ndikanononoka ndinochiona kumba uko ndandega.[9]*"*

As if the gift had not knocked Vimba over, Panganai a man on a mission and eager to show how serious he was about being *samusha*[10] gave her a fraction of his savings instructing her to keep it. He would go back to work and save an additional sum to be able to marry her.

Charmed by his thoughtfulness and remarkable effort, the walls came crumbling down and the lovers gracefully let their souls and bodies collide.

Seven months passed without hearing from Panganai and yet she had been eagerly waiting to share the good news she bore. Left with no choice, wearing her heart on a sleeve, Vimbai felt compelled to ask his family regarding his whereabouts. Upon asking, she learnt that the man she was in love with and for whom she was carrying a child for had joined the guerrilla force. Numbed with shock and out of solutions, disclosing the secret to her mother was the only way forward as she was the only one who could help her through her dilemma. As for Shewe, she was certain he was going to be disappointed in her. As if him beating her into pulp would not be enough, he was probably going to ask her to dig a pit, throw herself in it and bury her.

"Vimbai how do we tell that man? We are done for my child," lamented MaSiziba as she threw her hands above her head, bowed in surrender, clutched in her stomach and at her thighs. Finally, her knees gave in and she just sprawled herself on the floor next to her daughter in dismay.

---

[9] Do not ill-advise me, if I get back home late I will be in trouble

[10] head of the house

"But mama he wouldn't elope, he'll come back I know he will."

"*Mwamwa mwi mwimwi mwi mwanyo*[11]. He will, huh? Not only are you foolish but you are also naïve. *Heee*[12]! With this mess you have made you even have the nerve to back chat, I will…," she scoffed as she stood up raising her hand towards her daughter then she resisted the urge to slap her. Whilst still standing she resumed to poking Vimbai's forehead with her index finger and she continued, "…you should just shut up." She left the room mumbling to herself, "of all men imagine a whole guerrilla *mxxm*[13] this child."

MaSiziba was beside herself from learning that her daughter was expecting. Despite her furious outburst she still had quite the mountain to climb; the greatest dare which would be to inform her husband. Hesitant to tell her husband of their daughter's scandal time passed as she kept on procrastinating until she decided to disclose it to *Tete*[14] *Vee*, Shewe's sister from whom the name Vimbai had come from. She was easier to approach and probably wiser in these circumstances. Tete would know how best to talk to her brother and to discuss the way forward with regards to the issue. MaSiziba sent a message with her younger sister calling for Tete; asking her to come as she had an urgent matter that needed to be addressed in her presence.

When Tete Vee came, it was just before lunch and fortunately Shewe was not around. After serving her with

---

[11] Mocking her with sounds

[12] What

[13] Anger sound

[14] aunt, sister to the father

a plate of food, MaSiziba left Tete in the round thatch-roofed kitchen to delight herself and went to look for her daughter. MaSiziba's intention was to inform Vimbai regarding what she was planning on (involving Tete Vee to help discuss the issue with Shewe).

On entering Vimbai's room, she was stunned to see her daughter mourning and groaning on the floor.

"Vimbai," she screamed and ran towards her. As she wondered what was happening her mind raced for the wildest thoughts.

"Mama I can't hold it anymore," mouthed Vimbai in great agony.

"Vimbai talk to me, what happened, what did you take? Speak!"

"I took nothing mama, it started in the *mmh argggghhhhhh* mama, it hurts!"

When she saw the spots of blood on the floor, she realized that the matter was out of hand for her to handle. At the top of her voice, she called for Shewe's sister.

Upon hearing MaSiziba's call Tete ran to Vimbai's room.

"*Gogoi, komakanaka here munhanaga umo*[15]?" said Tete Vee as she entered Vimbai's room. "*Muroora*[16]!" cried out Tete astounded by the sight of the state of her brother's daughter.

"Tete, please help I don't know what's going on with her."

Upon seeing that Vimbai's pain was no ordinary pain, she bent down and reached for her niece so as to comfort

---

[15] Knock knock. Is everything well there?

[16] Daughter in law or sister-in-law

and support her. Hurriedly MaSiziba explained to Tete the whole situation. Despite being shocked with the news, she was present and had to play her role. Being an elder with somewhat commendable experience on assisting with child birth, she ordered MaSiziba to bring a basin filled with warm water, a towel and a bed sheet as she held her niece.

They carried Vimbai on to the bed. Tete Vee dabbed the towel into the basin and applied it on to Vimbai's lower back, and placed the sheet under Vimbai's buttocks. "*Muroora kasika, enda unosheedza nyamukuta*[17]," she ordered.

Traditionally the elderly women known to have the experience and expertise of assisting women with birthing of a child and delivering in labour are referred to as *Nyamukuta*. When MaSiziba returned with *Nyamukuta*, Vimbai's womb was letting go the foetus.

She began pushing and ultimately a sturdy lively baby entered the world with a cry. Untimely, the secret was revealed!

The birth of a child, especially a boy in the Shona culture was rendered an achievement as they would continue the family name into the next generation. It was traditionally associated with joy and a call for celebration. Unfortunately, not in the case of Vimbai's baby. She bore him out of wedlock thus making him an illegitimate child, a child of a soldier and an absent father. This would compromise the principles that their family stood up for. Such news would be the downfall of Shewe's highly esteemed reverence in the village. The courageous freedom fighters were admired by the community as people had endured enough suppression, and so were the

---

[17] Quickly daughter-in-law, go and call the traditional midwife

missionary delegates too. Nonetheless, the two groups of influence were societally separated.

This would also scar MaSiziba's marriage. She was responsible for keeping an eye on the daughters. Shewe would blame her for letting Vimbai go astray under her watch and not instilling enough discipline to set her on the straight and narrow.

Folded with pity as well as disappointment Tete began, "Koiwe[18] Vimbai, what kind of nonsense is this?"

Vimbai had no response to Tete's question and in justification of herself when she fell pregnant Panganai had not yet joined the freedom fighters force, instead they had plans of marriage. However, she kept quiet with her head bent and eyes fixed to the bed that she sat on.

After a while of silence and cluelessness whilst holding her wrapped up grandson in her arms MaSiziba broke the silence, "What should we do now Tete?"

"I have never seen nor heard of this," Tete Vee clapped her hands as she responded with so much rage. The traditional midwife was asked to leave as they had to attend to a family matter in private.

"Vimbai, if Panganai never comes back do you understand what's at stack here? Your future! You'll live a spinster's life till you die because of this child. No sane man would take his cows to pay lobola for a woman who has a child."

Vimbai did not know how to respond to her aunt. Filled with embarrassment quietly she clutched onto the warm impala blanket they had covered her with after her labour. Tete was older and wiser than MaSiziba, she would know how to best address this situation hence they dared

---

[18] as for you

not to interrupt her and paid attention to what she would instruct them to do.

"Now you are quiet. Am I talking to myself or maybe I'm the one who is crazy? I just like talking to myself in a room with people. Is that so?"

Vimbai's unresponsiveness was beginning to frustrate Tete; if they were going to resolve this matter, she had to avoid Tete being angry. Reluctantly, she responded, "No Tete."

"Isn't it you see yourself woman enough?"

"No Tete."

"*Iyaa.*"

"No Tete."

"*Bwoo* Tete *Bwoo*. You! You are confused my brother's daughter. Let me make things clear and easy for you. Yes! You see yourself woman enough *ne16 years idzodzo*[19]*;* you couldn't keep your legs closed and we are here sitting with a baby whose father we do not even know if he is going to come back or not. *Sisi* [20]he is at war where people fight, in the process some live and some die. If he dies there it means you'll never know the pleasure of a man for the rest of your life, is that what you want? MaSiziba tell her."

She had to respond and say something to acknowledge her presence. Embarrassed, lowly MaSiziba responded, "*Zvakaoma tete, ibasa*[21]."

"*Newe unazvo muroora, mwana kuzvimba kudai*[22], she was even going to get to full term and deliver without you telling anyone."

---

[19] With the 16 years that you have

[20] sister

[21] It is very difficult to handle this aunt

[22] You are also to blame; the child is heavily pregnant as is

She was raging. Responding would give her more ammunition so silently and attentively they let her speak. For a while the room was occupied by a muzzle, then Tete stood up and began pacing across the room. When she walked towards the window with her arms folded, she starred observantly through the window as if she saw someone coming; it could have been Shewe. She turned, looked at Vimbai first. Then turned to MaSiziba who was scared and curiously looking at Tete wondering if he had already returned home. Tete walked across the room and took a seat on the corner of the bed and began,

"*Nyaya yakaoma iyi*[23], very difficult for me to think of a better solution this is what is going to happen here, not a word to Shewe about all of this. MaSiziba we are going to clean up this room and your stray daughter. Afterwards, immediately at dusk, *Mainini*[24] Rugare (MaSiziba's sister) and Vimbai will wrap the baby in a warm blanket put him in the farm basket and take him to Mushamhuru."

Mushamhuru was a big stream that flowed through the proximity of the village separating it from the nearby village of Nyamhere. It was a significant tributary to the extensive Odzi river.

"Leave him in between the reeds, run and return back home, do not look back."

September 1979

---

[23] this is a difficult issue

[24] aunt, the younger sister to a mother

2 **All Hail Mukarpura**[25]

The ongoing busy streets of Harare initially gave me a fright. Embarrassed, I will confess that I got lost on my way to school countless times. Self-reassurance that with time I would eventually get used was my pillar of confidence. The traffic was hectic, chaos overwhelmed the streets with a deluge of pedestrians, the speeding *kombis*[26], unruly street kids, all this I found along my way to school. My father's brother, Uncle Nongai had taken me to school the first two weeks and as a responsible guardian he had asked me if I had mastered the roads. With the need to impress him and unwilling to trounce my ego I reassured him that I had.

After a few consecutive days of tailing fellow colleagues whom I attended the same school with I discovered a tip which would guide me. After getting off the kombi along Chinhoyi Street I would walk straight up

---

[25] the Cinnamomum Camphora tree

[26] commuter omnibuses

the road till I reached the Tokyo car sales garage in Samora Machel Avenue which, I marked more as the end of town where there was less commotion. Thus, it was less confusing and from there I would find my way to Allan Wilson Boys High School. It was a delightful experience to be given an opportunity to study at one of the most academically and sports competitive schools, considering my primary education background. I vowed to make the most out of this opportunity and make my parents proud.

My name is Mutsva which means new, from the village of Nyamhere and the only child to my parents. I was given this name by mama as an acknowledgement of being a new, unexpected and a pleasant addition to the family. I am an aspiring doctor; growing up I came to understand my purpose as being a care giver, one who ensures a healthy outcome to the unwell. I realized this when my maternal grandmother fell ill. She developed a wound behind her left knee which made it difficult and painful for her to bend her leg when walking. As a result, my father suggested that she had to stay with us so we could support and assist her.

I loved Gogo but I could not stand the smell of her wound. Telling my mother or anyone about it would just come across as disrespectful and insensitive; not that they could not smell the awful odour too but there was just nothing that could be done about it besides washing it. She had been given medication at the clinic to alleviate her pain but Gogo hated taking the medication. She would either blatantly refuse to take it or would pseudo swallow it. I would often see her throw the pills out through the window. She knew that I knew but we just never spoke about it. She was a loving and caring grandmother and always great company but the smell of her wound really did a number on me. I would struggle to get to sleep because of the stench such that I started believing that I was inhaling it all till it intoxicated me and drowsed me to sleep.

Whilst in the bushy mountains herding goats with my peers my eyes caught sight of a peculiar green plant which had expansive, broad leaves and had tiny black balls suspended from the plant branches. It smelt so good that I plucked it out with the intention of spreading it onto Gogo's wound. Perhaps the beautiful smell would dilute that of the wound. I was excited to have found an antidote, only to wake up and realise that it had just been a dream. For a week the same dream kept on recurring, I was so drunk on this wound's smell that I even dreamt Gogo asking me when I would show her my surprise plant.

Chamuka and Maneta were my friends with whom I went herding. Whilst on our herding expedition in the mountain called Nerimiti, Maneta had one stubborn goat that was ever trying to flee from the rest of the tribe. As I was tying it to a hardwood, I saw the same plant that I had repeatedly dreamt of but a little further from where I was. Immediately, after tying up the goat I ran to it and yes it smelled just as good as it had in my dream. Excited, I plucked out a few leaves and threw them into the plastic bag which had my packed lunch. Being a mere 5 years old infant, I had no idea of how I was going to convince mama and Gogo to put this into Gogo's wound without coming across as impolite.

Every evening before retiring to sleep mama would wash Gogo's wound. Instead, I offered to wash Gogo's wound. They should have thought I was the most adorable grandchild yet I had my own intentions. I grinded the leaves, they did not exactly become powder fine as they were too fresh but they were small enough. I would put on the sweet-smelling juice on to the towel which I would use to wiped Gogo's wound. I took longer cleaning her wound than mama did; besides my hands being small and I being slower it was because of my secret addition. It was a tedious process for the poor old woman but if it would help, it had to be done.

I continued plucking off this plant as it was working magically, the smell had vanished. Chamuka grew curious and started questioning me on my sudden plant plucking habit. Not willing to embarrass my grandmother, I resolved to covering it up by setting off and commenced a new hobby; cuniculture practice. I would use the rabbits as scapegoats, the reason why I had begun plucking greens. Excited with my newly found hobby my friends began joining me; they would pluck out whatever green plant they came across. They would even pay visits to come and feed my rabbits, poor mammals were being overfed by the overzealous young champs.

Weeks passed and it officially became my prime responsibility to clean Gogo's wound. She even disclosed to me that she preferred my cleaning because I cleaned it gently and I removed all the dirt evidenced by the absence of the foul smell. It was a pleasant compliment and also confirmation that my remedy was working, I ratified it too as I was beginning to sleep better. Fascinatingly the plant did not only eliminate the smell from the wound, it was also gradually bringing the skin tissues close together. In spite of this I was only focused on getting rid of the smell and barely paid attention to the plant's other effects till one day when I returned home from herding goats.

Gogo was sitting on the reeds mat under the huge mango tree. Impossible I thought, as she could hardly stand let alone walk and mama could not have lifted her up. As for baba, he would not even go as far as touch Gogo's hand because of the traditional boundaries of in-law's respect. How?

It was not my place to ask so I did not. However, I was happy to see her outside. If she was able to walk, then it meant she had recovered and was no longer ill. I greeted Gogo and went inside the house, assured that with my mama's loudness I would find out. She would definitely, eagerly, share with anyone how Gogo had ended up under the shed. The foul odour was long gone; I missed it when I could not fall asleep because I no longer had anything to blame for keeping me awake. Gogo's ability to move once again made me realise that the plant also had healing properties. I did not mention anything about using the plant lest I got into trouble.

On one Sunday afternoon when Baba and I returned from church, I was surprised to see a lot of people in our yard. It was then when I learnt of the worst and mind shuttering news that whilst we were away Gogo had passed on. I could not understand, what could have caused her death? She seemed to have been getting better. Just when I was considering finding ways to plant that leaf I used to clean her wound on the yard for easier access, tragedy had struck.

I began to wonder if the plant I had been using had killed Gogo; it might have had poison and the more I had used it, the more poison I had deposited into her body. Clouded by guilt and grief I thought to myself—what had I done? I should have left the wound to heal naturally on its own and the foul smell would eventually stop. Instead, the foul smell left and took my Gogo along with it. I felt the need to disclose to my parents what I had been doing despite the fact that I was scared.

Baba sought to give Gogo a dignified send off. Before burial she was taken to the mortuary where a post mortem was done in order to give closure to the family concerning her sudden death. The doctor who used to come visit Gogo together with a nurse who dispensed her medication came with the results of the post mortem in which we learnt that Gogo had cancer. She had been aware but had not disclosed the diagnosis to us. It had spread into her bones; her medication had been for delaying migration of the cancer in her body system. Since she despised taking the medication, which only I knew, the illness had spread fast claiming her life and prematurely taking her away from us.

After Gogo's burial, I struggled to sleep wondering how I would begin telling my parents about the plant I had used to wash Gogo's wound. The thought of disappointing them and hurting mama troubled me. I prayed and hoped that they would understand that it was not an act of mischief, rather, a considerate act for wellness.

Then I dreamt of Gogo; with a smile she approached me. This dream was definitely a subject of my guilt. She was holding the leaves of the plant I had used to wash her wound with, she took my right hand smiling still without saying a word and she placed the stalks of the leaves into the palm of my hands and pushed my fingers over the stalks. As she was walking away, I cried out to her apologising and she turned to face me and said:

'Mutsva, you did well and you did what you were called to do. You are a bigger person than you or any of those around you could ever see because of the gift within you. They know you but they don't know you.'

The deep words she said were difficult for me to comprehend. Nonetheless the smile she gave me set me free from feeling guilty. I was not responsible for her death so I decided not to disclose anything to my parents.

3 They see the bush; I see my sanctuary

As I was doing seventh grade, my registration to write the national examinations got delayed because I did not have a birth certificate. I could not understand why it had taken my parents that long to obtain my birth certificate; it had been twelve years since I had been born. Surely, they had had enough time to apply for it. Out of curiosity I decided to ask my mother. It was then when I knew that I was not biologically born into my family.

Mama had been married to my father for four years and unfortunately had failed to conceive. They were childless until one early morning when she had gone to do her laundry kwaMushamhuru and she found me in the reeds. Learning of the story made me grow more grateful as I could have not asked for a better mother than her let alone an incredible father I had in her husband. Baba had tried with all the possible connections he had to pull strings that I may get a birth certificate. However, our village town was a bit behind with civilization, the efficiency of the system was poor. As a result, I could not register for the grade 7 national examinations.

When my peers began writing the national examinations, devastated I stopped going to school. Staying at home whilst other children of my age headed for school did not sit well with my mother; she would be filled with pity and guilt at the sight of me moving about the homestead. I had often reminded her that it was not her fault but she would still feel terrible. To save her from the self-torture I decided to spend my days wondering around in the bushy mountains keeping myself occupied with hunting, herding the goats and doing anything that would seem interesting then find my way back home at sunset.

Funny how I was comfortable with being alone in the bush, the forest had just opened its arms and embraced me. Effortlessly, the trees, the grass; nature basically became my greatest companion. I would vent to them, ask for their opinions and even share jokes with them. Though their laughter was not as audible as mine, being in the forest soothed my troubled spirit. I felt a sense of belonging just like being at home.

It was in October the season of *Mupfura*[27] the world famous Amarula. On that fateful day I let up all my frustration on to the fruits. After delighting myself my head felt lightened and my eyes heavy, I was filled with euphoria. I could hardly walk; the ground was sloppy I could not maintain my balance. I reached for a huge brown rock, were I decided to take a seat. It felt so nice and warm and there I lay my back. The sky looked beautifully blue with no clouds, that is all I saw and I fell

[27] the Amarula tree

asleep. A loud scream or rather cry awakened me, it sounded like a cry of panic and pain. I instantly sobered up and ran towards the sound of the cry. I was not scared; I was rather surprised and curious to find out what could have possibly happened for someone to be in such despair in my sanctuary.

I got to where the sobs were coming from and there, I saw a young girl sitting down holding her left foot ankle. Next to her was a long thick old machete. From the smell that came from the wound on her ankle I could tell the type of snake that had bitten her. A serpent's poison when mixed with blood gives a certain scent; it was a Hognose that had bitten her. I had witnessed Hognose bites from one of my peers whom I had walked with home from school. As their bites were small and shallow the poison would take a while to absorb its way to contaminate the blood flow in the major blood vessels. I had learnt about this in environmental science. As for knowing the smell, even I myself could never really explain that. We were in the midst of the bush; the village was far and the clinic even further. I had not seen her before so obviously I would not know where she stayed. Therefore, I assumed she lived in another village. Faced with this crisis I was obliged to do something immediately to save her life as she would not make it to the clinic.

From the Tilia tree which was used to tie firewood, I pulled a fresh bark. Just above her ankle I tied an airtight note to prevent the poison from moving into any veins and just below her ankle I used the machete to cut off the blood flow that was contaminated. I had never experienced or witnessed any treatment of a snake bite, I had no idea what I was doing but my mind and hands were in sync and working frantically, all I had to do was oblige.

She was astounded by what I was doing although hesitant to ask as she was desperate for any help that would sustain her life so she gladly accepted mine. I was glad she did not ask because had she done so my mouth would have deceived my mind and hands that were doing very strange and yet familiar work.

Just as everything good has a complementary bad the same goes for smells. I needed to find a plant which produced a smell that complemented the one coming from her wound. I was determined to look for it and find it, just like I did for Gogo's wound; not only had the plant solved the odour crisis but also healed her wound. Perhaps the reason a plant would produce a smell complementary to that from the snake bite would be to weaken the poison and reduce its toxicity. I searched around but to my disappointment I could not find any.

Defeated, I returned and carried her to the clinic. We got to the clinic and found it closed. I did not know what else to do to save the poor girl. She could see how helpless I was when we both witnessed our doom.

"Don't worry yourself too much, you have helped me and done a lot already. If it wasn't for you, I might have not even survived till now," she said breaking the silence, as she saw the anxious look on my face.

"I won't be able to forgive myself if things turn out for the worst," I sincerely responded. I was disappointed with myself and I felt sorry for her.

As the evening wore it was getting dark; I had to get back home before mama got worried and baba returned. Baba had often reminded me that he would be the only one last to get home. I had no intention of defying him and endure the consequences. I felt challenged, she looked young, perhaps my age and yet I had to go home, and so did she.

In our conversing, I managed to gather that Miriro was her name, an orphan who relied on the care of her grandmother. She had moved into the neighbouring village of Chengetai following her parents passing; the living conditions at her grandmother's home impelled her to drop out of school. In my village, educating the girls was never prioritized because it was believed that they learnt of their future responsibilities from home and not from school. She seemed unbothered with missing out on school unlike me.

"So, what do you think should happen now?"

"I'm worried that it's getting late, I have to be home before baba."

"I will sleep here and wait till tomorrow when the clinic opens; they'll attend to me. It's okay you can go home."

"Leave you to sleep here alone?"

"Yes. It's fine. I'll be okay. It's not like the snake will come back to finish me off," she said with a smile trying to make me feel less remorse.

"You never know," I dumbly responded. I reassured her that I recognized her effort to make me feel better. Still, I was not going to be like my supposed mother, to just abandon her entrusting another anonymous to take the responsibility of finding her and helping her. I thought of taking her home with me; mama would help me watch over her.

"Miriro, so this is my suggestion on what we could do. You should come home with me; the earlier we go, the better, before my father gets home. Mama is a good person; she'll help care for your leg and we will bring you to the clinic tomorrow."

"Mutsva it's okay; I'll be fine here. I don't want you to get into trouble with your father because of me."

"I'll not get into trouble if you agree to come with me now but I'll definitely get into trouble if you take long to agree to come with me or if you refuse to come with me. Because, then I'll have to sleep here too as there's no way I'll leave and abandon you to sleep here alone," I responded frankly.

"Fine let's go but I'll never forgive myself if your father gets angry at you when he finds out about my presence in his yard."

"You don't have to worry about that," I said reaching for her hand and helped her stand and climb on to my back.

When we got home, we went and joined mama in the kitchen as she was preparing dinner and I explained to her what had transpired. Mama removed the tree bark, washed her leg, replaced it with a much neater piece of cloth, gave her food and prepared a comfortable place for her to sleep in the kitchen.

We sat and chatted but not for long because baba had to find us in the living room with the kitchen already locked up. He enjoyed having his supper in the kitchen as it was warmer but unfortunately, he had to miss that and mama said she would cover it up.

Mama was not happy that I was asking her to keep a secret from baba but she was kind enough to understand Miriro's situation. Dreading baba's questions on how I had kept myself busy during the day I went to sleep early.

Miriro stretched her hands towards my face and held my cheeks with her soft and warm hands. She looked straight into my eyes for long. It was strange and I just wanted to close my eyes but instead I starred at hers too.

Both of us did not say anything until she closed hers and said,

"Thank you Mutsva, you have shown me great kindness I'll never forget your care for me. You'll make a good doctor."

I would have asked her how she had unlocked the kitchen door or entered into the house let alone found my room but that was not important, my focus was on her. As she walked out, I noticed she was not limping.

"Mutsvaaaa, Mutsvaaaa," screamed mama as she woke me up.

How disappointing now, I had to face the reality of dealing with this worrisome snake bite.

She opened my door in panic and her face washed with worry. "She is gone Mutsva. Miriro is gone."

What was she talking about? I wondered. Hurriedly, I got up and followed her to the kitchen and yes, she had left!

"I came to the kitchen immediately after your father left and found the door unlocked, blankets folded and neatly arranged in a pile but she was not here."

4 Relocation

My birth certificate was finally issued a year later, therefore, I had to repeat grade seven. I loved and enjoyed school; repeating what I had previously learnt made it possible for me to attain excellent marks in the examinations. Impressed with my results, Uncle Nongai suggested that I proceed with my secondary education in Harare. I had never been anywhere else beyond the city of Mutare. I dreaded the thought of having to adjust to a new environment in addition to a new school.

"Mutsva it will be a brilliant idea for you to go to Harare. There are more opportunities in the big city," Baba parroted uncle's words, trying to convince me as he noticed my reluctance. With the intention to reassure me, he would continue with his monotonous reasoning, "Better for you to go there whilst you're still young, you'll adjust well compared to going there when you are older."

Frankly speaking, I really had no choice; I was obliged to comply with the plans of the elders as they supposedly knew and wanted what was best for me.

A week before the holidays had ended, I joined Uncle Nongai and his family on their trip back to Harare. Schools were set to open in January. Relocating was a venture of adjustment for me. Uncle Nongai and his family stayed in the small location of Dzivarasekwa. Aunty Maggie, his wife, was very accommodating; she made room for me by asking her two daughters to share one bedroom. Mitchell, the youngest aged six, had to move to her sister's room, Mellissa who was four years' older. In turn, I was given Mitchell's room. Yes, this was a family of English names. I would call Aunty Maggie 'mainini' as my mother did. Fortunately, the girls' names were called in short Mimi was Mitchell and Meme was Mellissa, that was easy enough.

The routine of the day as I was settling in was as follows: Uncle Nongai and his wife would leave for work early in the morning leaving behind Meme, Mimi, the helper whom was named Sisi and I. We hardly engaged in any conversations with my cousins because most of their discussions were in regard with cartoons, TV drama, movies, soap operas, their school and their neighbours of which I knew nothing about all of that. I was used to waking up at the crack of dawn at home, but because I had no idea of what I would do if I were to leave my room that early I resumed to staying in bed till the sun was up. By the time I left my room Sisi would be done with cleaning the house and have breakfast prepared for my cousins and I.

There were no mountains nor forest around to which I could go and perhaps keep myself occupied during the day. I hated working in the field but I found myself weeding the yard; it was the only thing which seemed familiar to keep me occupied.

Soon as schools opened the waking up routine changed, everyone was given their bathing timeslot by mainini. Uncle Nongai was the first, followed by me, I had to wake up at 05:30 and be done by 05:45 followed by Mimi and Meme. Each of us was instructed to not spend more than a quarter of an hour in the bathing room.

Mainini would shower last as she would be busy preparing our lunch boxes to take to school and instructing Sisi on the things she needed done during the day. Mimi and Meme never adhered to the waking up schedules and mainini would take more time bathing. This saw us being late as we would leave the house at around 07:30. The hectic traffic at that hour would stretch the supposed 30 minutes' journey to the CBD to longer.

After two consecutive weeks of being late Uncle Nongai suggested that I use the kombis for me to be punctual; that is when I began taking the commuter omnibuses to town. I preferred sitting in the front seat, next to the driver so I could see the road as he drove. That way I would not have to contend with being squeezed by other passengers or endure the constant up and down and folding of the seat to make way for those at the back to exit the kombi; It was really a cumbersome exercise.

Sitting with the driver also saved my uniform from creasing. On the first day, the kombi trip seemed to be going well until people began calling out what appeared to be their drop off stops. With about five people left in the kombi, I calmly sat and continued the journey waiting for the conductor to tell us when we got to the final stop.

"Right, the driver stops here. *Pano ndopaperera mari yenyu vabereki*[28]!"

---

[28] the fare that you paid suffices only up to here

We had arrived at the final stop and like every other passenger I exited the kombi. As I was trying to figure out how to find my way, I read a green fingerboard hanged about three meters up the tower light, Chinhoyi street. I had no idea where to go from there. I had no other choice but to ask the kombi drivers and conductors.

Half of an hour passed and not one of them gave me directions to my school, they kept on making a joke out of my tone of speaking, how I had ironed my uniform and my mirror shining shoes. Seeing that I was not getting any help, politely I left them before I had wasted anymore of my time. Fortunately, I identified two guys in the uniform similar to mine, all black. I decided to follow them; regrettably they were not going to my school. I realized it when they stopped at a building with a banner written Christian College of Southern Africa. There were many of them, all in the black uniform and there were even girls too, my school was for boys only.

Distraught I continued down the road, the street sign protruding from a steel bar read 'Leopold Takawira Street'. The road from that point became swamped with more girls, some were dressed in the green and others blue tunic uniforms. Already this showed me I was lost. I resorted to asking once again. I dared not approach any of these girls lest they make a clown of me. I continued ahead till I got to the traffic lights. Herbert Chitepo was the name of the street I crossed. I asked the newspaper vendor who was sitting on the side of the road selling The Herald newspaper. Empathetically, he reassured me that I was not far from my school and he directed me.

Following his directions, I found my way to the school's gate. I was late and already there were prefects at the gate writing names of the late comers; a punishment awaited us at the end of the day. Unbothered by the punishment, I was relieved I had managed to find my way. I just wanted to get to class so I could sit down and rest my tired feet.

Tuesday, I got lost once again. I had tried to recall and follow the routes I had taken the previous day but unfortunately, I found myself asking for directions to my school again. Then after identifying a group of guys from my school whom I followed, eventually I mastered a route to school from Chinhoyi street. My uncle did not know of my struggles; I had not told him because I wanted him to see that I was confident, a high achiever and I needed to give him something to see that I was adjusting well to my new life, the city life.

I grew popular because of my accent. *Wasu*[29] was my given nickname from most of the kombi operators. Finding friends at school was not difficult, although they would make fun of my accent and some of my Shona terms but I settled well in school.

---

[29] nickname given to people from Manicaland

5 The Collision

The arrangement made when I began high school was that I would go home every December holiday. During the in between school term holidays, I would join my host family on their short family trips. It was then when I visited the magnificent Domboshava, sacred Chinhoyi caves and the beautiful Mazvikadei resort. Another holiday I remember we went to the home of stonework, the glorious Great Zimbabwe in Masvingo. During the Easter April holidays of my second year in High school we paid a visit to the resplendent smoke that thunders, Mosi-oa-Tunya and the following August holiday we went to the exuberant Mutarazi falls of Nyanga. Their zeal of travelling gave me the opportunity of exposure to all these resorts. For that reason, I was fortunate to witness the beautiful and ancient architecture of my country.

All the holidays I shared with them were packed with great memories and activities. Nonetheless, I was always expectant of my December holidays. Nothing could trade in place of with being with mama and baba.

One holiday when I went home, I found mama going through a stressful and worrisome time, her best friend

MaGumbo had not been well. She was on strict bed rest so mama would go and visit her daily.

One day she asked me to accompany her, she needed me to carry a parcel for her. Regardless of my presence in the room, MaGumbo removed the linen that she laid under, revealing her daunting wound. Unable to continue staring at it, I avoided relooking as everything about this wound reminded me of Gogo's wound, the smell the size and the tissue around it. Out of respect I excused myself from the room, leaving mama and her friend to have some space. By then, my mind was already in the bush. Perhaps I could get the expansive leaves of the muKapura tree and advise her to use it on to her wound as I had done for Gogo, but how could I convince her it worked? There would need to be some reassurance and it could not come from mama; I still had not disclosed to her about it.

As I sat under the shade of the spreading grape plantation, Matipa walked into sight. She was coming from the garden holding in her hand a basket containing green vegetables. Matipa was MaGumbo's youngest daughter, she was a year younger than me, a cheerful, well-mannered and hard-working girl. We got along well she was the sister I would had loved to have. Out of courtesy, we exchanged greetings. Immediately, I made space so we could share the stool I was sitting on. "Here sit we can fit."

"I hope these will be enough for all of you," she said, extending her hands to hand over the basket to me.

"That is very thoughtful of you Matipa and very kind also," I said, accepting the unexpected offering in response.

"Don't mention; this is less compared to what your mother has been doing for us."

"Still, I say you are kind and thoughtful. How have you been?"

"I have been okay, just having a tough time with mama being sick. If it wasn't for your mother Mutsva I really have no idea of what I would have done or have been now." At once a stream of tears ran down her chicks. Her pain was deeper beyond what words could express. It was not easy for her, to watch her mother lying helplessly in bed with no desired will of life.

MaGumbo was in pain and as much as I did not want to think of the worst, I feared the prognosis of MaGumbo's illness; it was going to affect her daughter. I wanted to help my little sister, I had to help her. It would haunt me knowing I did nothing to help. Just as I hugged her, the silently falling tears snowballed into a lurid agonizing cry. Tighter I clasped her to reassure her that I felt what she could not say. After she had calmed down, I asked to take her for a walk. We walked to the mountain, Gomo Nerimiti. I was taking her to the healing plant. We both walked quietly I had so many questions I wanted to ask her but I could tell that she was not eager to engage in a conversation.

"Thank you for this."

"Don't mention, it's the least I can do. Tell me Matipa where is your older sister and her twin brother?"

"Sisi is married, she lives with her husband in Chiredzi and she is also working there. She does come to visit but when she does, she can't be here for long and *mukoma*[30] Tonde is in Botswana that's where he is working and also settled with his family. So yeah, they really can't be here all the time, it's my role to take."

---

[30] Big brother

"You're doing very well taking care of MaGumbo. I'm sure she is happy and grateful to have you by her side."
"She is but at times she feels overwhelmed by the pain and she says hurtful things. She wills to die Mutsva. What will I do without mama?"

Again, she began to cry. This is what I was trying to avoid. We were close to where I was taking her but I had to calm her down, so I drew her to seat on the stone and I rubbed her back for consolation.

"When Sisi came to visit we took her to the clinic and we were given medication. Initially, she was taking it then she began refusing to take it, she is giving up and I don't know how to help her. I need her…," cried Matipa as she spoke with so much anger.

"…I've heard of some natural remedies such as *Mupangara*[31]. I was told that it has small fruits that you burn and use the ashes to apply to a wound. It heals the wound. And another called *Mukombegwa*[32]. I need to find them and try; might work."

Things have a way of working themselves out.
Unaware Matipa had opened the key discussion I had intended to have with her. After allowing her to calm down, I told her all about Gogo's wound and how I had cleaned it. Since she was keen to know, I took her to the tree and we took from it leaves enough to last a while and we went ahead to look for the Mupangara tree and Mukombegwa. It was then I realized how Gomo Nerimiti had the most worthwhile trees. This explained why it was said to be a sacred mountain and famous plateau.

---

[31] The dichrostachys cinerea tree or Kalahari Christmas tree

[32] the common crown- berry tree

As mama continued with her daily check-ups on her friend, not a single day did she come back with exciting news concerning MaGumbo's wellbeing. I tried being patient but I was curious. In view of the fact that I could not just go there, I had to wait for mama to send me or ask me to accompany her or fortunately come across Matipa in the walks around the village.

Two more weeks passed with none of that happening and my holiday eventually ended. I did not want to put pressure on Matipa to tell me or give her false hope but before I left for Harare, I went to MaGumbo's house to bid them farewell. I went with mama and as usual MaGumbo exposed her wound whilst I was still in the room. I could not resist the urge to look, her wound was neatly drying up and healing. The huge septic hole was closing up. As I left mama behind with MaGumbo, Matipa and I walked to the gate.

"Mutsva I'm so glad that mama is getting better, when you return on your next holiday, I'm certain you'll see her walking around," she said with relief displayed in her small shiny eyes.

I was pleased and relieved to know that the outcome looked positive. Seeing Matipa in such a good spirit was satisfying. After sharing words of encouragement and a goodbye hug, with great fulfilment I left home for Harare.

For a change, during the short April school term holiday, Uncle Nongai decided that we visit my homestead. The Easter holidays collectively with the national independence holiday were more ideal as it would see an opportunity for Uncle No and mainini to have days off from work. I was very excited and looked forward to seeing mama and baba. We got home just before midnight. After we had prayed thanking God for the travelling mercies, mama told me she would prepare for me to sleep in the kitchen. I believed she had reserved my bedroom for Mimi and Meme.

Early in the morning, soon as I woke up, I went to the living room to get my toiletry bag. I had not managed to put away my bag so I had left it behind the sofa. To my surprise I found Meme and Mimi folding blankets. They had slept in the living room and not my bedroom! Knowing my cousins, they would not have slept on the ground by choice. I wondered then for whom mama had reserved my bedroom. Uncle Nongai and mainini had their own small room that baba had built for this purpose that when they come to visit, they may have their own dignified space. So, there was no way they were sleeping in my room. We exchanged morning greetings but because of curiosity I went ahead to peep into my room. To my surprise, there was someone sleeping on my bed. I was not sure but the figure seemed as that of a girl.
She was not going to sleep for the whole day, I told myself. I would eventually learn of who she was as the day went by. So, I slowly closed the door.

As I was heading back to the living room, mama came out of her bedroom. She looked at me as if I was in trouble. I had not trespassed—that was my bedroom so in defence I spoke out of turn, "Morning mama, who is sleeping in my room?"

"Did you not see?"

"No, I did not," I responded impatiently.

"Come," she said holding my hand pulling me into her bedroom.

As usual baba being the early bird of the house, had already left. It could have been for work or for whatever that was too important for him to not be able to sleep for long.

"It's Matipa. I asked baba to take her in as we wait for her brother to come and take her."

"I don't understand, what about MaGumbo who is she with?" I think I already knew the answer but I could not get to accept it without mama confirming it.

"My friend rested mwanangu. She fought her part of the battle and it was time," responded mama with a broken voice.

I did not know how I could comfort her. She seemed to have done that enough for herself. Her spirit was daunted by her friend's death. If she was like this, what more Matipa? I wanted to avoid her and as there were so many new faces around the house, I was certain she would also hesitate to come out. I sympathized with her for her loss but awkwardly I did not know what I would do or say to make her feel better. This was way beyond me, especially upon remembering what she had said to me the last time we had met. With the prime intention being to avoid Matipa and the loud environment of the four women around the homestead, I left the house.

I decided to pay a visit to my friends Chamuka and Maneta. Once they knew I was home, we would go together anywhere. Chamuka was busy behind the kitchen breaking firewood when I got to his house. His mother was the first to see me. She greeted me with so much cheer and took me to where he was. He had the company of his two younger sisters, the two chatterboxes. Lucky him I used to think but after staying with Meme and Mimi I realized I dreaded how they would not stop talking. Of the two beautiful sisters, Rugare was the oldest and was also a good friend of Matipa, most interestingly she admired Maneta. Sadly because of the 'bro code' between my friends it did not allow for anything to happen.

After engaging with them all in a short conversation, Chamuka and I left for Maneta's house. From Maneta's house I had to find my way back home. I had accomplished my mission; with my friends aware I was around they would not forget to come and take me with them to any errands. When I got home baba and Uncle No were sitting under the huge mango tree that Gogo used to enjoy sitting under. I went to greet them and I proceeded to the kitchen where the four ladies were busy preparing food as it was almost lunch time. I did not fit to join either of these two groups. I left the kitchen clueless of what to do with myself. Until it hit me that Matipa needed someone to console and confide in. There honestly was nothing I could do to make her feel better but avoiding her was unjustifiable. I took it on the chin, found my way to my bedroom. The closer I got my feet became heavy. Suddenly, I doubted my intentions and made a U-turn with the intention to rather join baba and babamunini.

"Mutsva," she called as I headed towards the door.

I was not ready to face her. I ridiculed myself for coming into the house. I could have avoided this awkward moment. "I was on my way to check on you but thought you were resting and I need not disturb you."

"Oh, I see; more of avoiding me."

"You know I wouldn't," I lied through my teeth walking towards her. Just as I held her in my arms, she broke into unfathomable moans. The obliviousness of death, it takes, regardless of the pain it causes to those who remain. The only thing I presumed could make her feel better was to have her mother back but I could never be able to do that nor was it even possible. If I were to lose my mother; unimaginable! At that thought I felt a sharp stabbing pain. Is this what Matipa was going through? As I tightly embraced her in one arm, I used my right arm to rub her back consoling her but it barely made any impact on her weeping. "I'm so sorry for the loss Matipa," I whispered as I kept consoling her. I did not say it once I said it a couple of times until she pushed herself off my chest.

"I'm so sorry I didn't mean to put you in such an awkward space. I just can't find words to express myself. The only way I'm able to express myself is by crying."

"It's alright I totally understand and it's okay you know you can be yourself with me. Come take a seat. You need to stay out of that room; you need the air," I said as I took her hand to seat on our well-maintained old maroon tuscan leather sofas which Uncle No had gotten for my parents. Just as we sat down mama came in with two full plates.

"Wonderful Matipa! I'm glad someone could convince you out of that room," she stated as she put the plates on the coffee table in the midst of the room.

I turned to Matipa looking forward to hearing her response. She responded with a shy smile; the sympathy was embarrassing her.

"Thank you Mutsva; you have no idea how relived I am to see her out," said mama smiling and then turned her face to focus on me. "You won't believe who is here."

"Who is it," I responded knowing that I had seen Chamuka and Maneta earlier on and there was nothing going on that day.

She stood by the door and called out, "Mirri, Mirri!".

Quietly, we waited to see the failed guess. We heard fast paced steps and at once she entered into the living room with a courteous smile.

"*Hesi* Mutsva?"

I could not believe my eyes! It was Miriro! In flesh and looking way better than when I had last seen her. She had mysteriously taken off after being bitten by the snake. I was thrilled to see her! After introducing her to Matipa, we shared the food. As we ate and chatted Matipa was withdrawn and ate less.

I got drawn into the conversation with Miriro because I wanted to find out what had happened to her after she left and it was also an opportunity to know more about her. I remembered Matipa was grieving and this was not the space she needed. I felt bad for forgetting to accommodate her and when I looked at her, she was enviously looking at Miriro. "Are you okay," I asked with the intention to break the awkward space.

"I'm alright," she answered and politely she continued, "excuse me I'm going to leave you two to catch up on old times. Nice to meet you Sisi." With a croaky smile to Miriro, she stood and left.

6 The Break

In 1995, Uncle Nongai advised me to stay behind during the end of year school holidays and attend extra lessons so as to maximise my chances of obtaining flying colours in my "O" level exams. It was an all-study holiday with no fun. I drew all of my focus towards schoolwork, assignments, extra lessons, and exam papers revision. I had a reputation to sustain--- that of a brilliant and intelligent son.

14 November 1996, I wrote my last examination paper, officially completing my secondary education. I was excited to eventually go home. On the 18th early in the morning Uncle Nongai took me to Mbare. I boarded the 06:00 bus to Chipinge. It was the furthest town the straight bus would get to and fortunately my bus stop was along the way. My journey ended at Sambare bus stop; a growth point, it consisted of a cluster of small-scale commercial stores.

Baba had been notified by his brother of my travelling. As I was getting off the bus, I saw Chamuka on the other side of the road through the window. He was already waiting for me with a cow driven cart. I supposed Baba had assigned him to come and fetch me. I was surprised to see him alone; Chamuka would hardly do errands without Maneta. The bus departed soon after offloading my luggage. He came over to where I was standing with my throng of luggage.

"Eee *mukomana*[33], welcome back. You were really studying hard; you look as if the wind can blow you away."

As always, the sarcastic joker. "Then you will carry these bags alone, because clearly I bear no muscles for anything heavy."

"Your luggage your burden, actually get on it at least I brought the car."

I laughed at his blunt refusal to help with my luggage, knowing that he really had no choice. I carried two of my bags and crossed the road leaving him behind with the heavier bags, one of it had the groceries I was sent to bring home. He followed behind me drudging his way to the cart with my other bags. He was stubborn but I could confidently rely on his aid.

"That wasn't too hard. You have enough weight for all of us," with a pat on the bag, I sarcastically commented.

"You will pay for this," he said with a straight face. For a moment he forgot that I knew of his ways.

"On top of what baba has already paid you? Not a chance. Climb on let's go I'm so homesick."

"Not so fast. There is still one more bag. Get your bag.

I'll climb on and wait for you. Chop *mukomana*."

"If Maneta were here, I wouldn't have to do so much work," I said as I loaded the last bag onto the cart and

---

[33] Young man

climbed in. Curious to find out where his partner in crime was. I rephrased my inquisitiveness, "Maneta *uripi*[34]," I said as I climbed into the cart.

"He is a waste of space that one. It's just you and me left now."

"I don't understand, what do you mean?"

"Maneta disappointed me. He betrayed the bro code. Of all the girls he chose to impregnate Rugare." His voice was filled with rage.

I was no expert on love so I could not understand why Maneta would do something to break the brotherhood we had. On the other hand, I thought to myself Chamuka needed to relax; he was not going to end up marrying Rugare, she was going to be married to another man anyway. Better it being a man close to him; at least he could be able to constantly check on his sister; but what did I know? I did not want to agitate him any further so I neither asked nor said anything more to him all the way home. It was a long and unpleasant ride. Was this how my holiday would be, having to choose between my two brothers from childhood, a friendship I held so dearly? I hated the idea of us never being together.

When I got home, Matipa was no longer staying with us. Mama told me her brother had taken her. Remembering that she had mentioned that her brother stayed in Botswana, I concluded I was never going to see her again. What was left to remind me of her was their house which I passed often when I walked around and her mother, MaGumbo's grave. MaGumbo had been laid to rest in the field within their yard.

---

[34] where is he

Mama told me Miriro had been paying her visits. We both still had no idea where she lived so I looked forward to seeing her whenever she was to visit mama again.

Chamuka and Maneta's dissension persisted. Chamuka was reluctant to engage in a conversation to resolve their conflict. I had to steal time to spend with Maneta without Chamuka knowing lest he felt betrayed. When paying Maneta a visit it was fulfilling to see the love he shared with Rugare and how she lightened up when talking to her husband; I wished for Chamuka to witness this, it would have put his rage at ease. On my first visit she seemed uncomfortable seeing me around their homestead, perhaps she thought I had come to spy for Chamuka because of the feud between her brother and her husband. She would shy away and avoid me. However, I noticed the growing potbelly; it could not be missed as her body had grown bigger as well.

When I returned from visiting Maneta's house, I overheard mama and baba having a conversation about me. Baba was complaining about how I was always on the road. To my defence mama scornfully asked him if he would have preferred that I marry her, as she was the only woman I could have known and loved if I were to stay indoors at once laughter covered the kitchen. I felt fulfilled witnessing the happiness my parents shared. I lived for moments like these.

It was a long and unlike what I had expected, the most distasteful holiday. I hardly got to spend time with both of my friends. The only highlight was spending time with my parents. I never thought I would do so but I began counting down days of my return to Harare. I guess I was looking forward to going back to school. I had put some thought into my future and was still sure of my decision to pursue medical studies.

Early January, Uncle Nongai was given a sponsored holiday vacation by his company. He intended to go with mainini, before leaving he paid us a visit. He came to ask for my parents' permission for me to return to Harare and keep watch over the house together with the girls during their absence. Eagerly I agreed, my holiday was vile, a change of scenery would make it better.

When I got to Harare, the following day Uncle Nongai and mainini left for their vacation leaving behind Mimi, Meme, Sisi and I. They were not strict and authoritarian but their absence just enlightened the space. Perhaps it was because there was no one to scrutinize our behaviour, speech, chores, eating patterns and sleeping routine.

When living on borrowed freedom you ought to maximize the opportunity. Sisi would get her work done early and leave the house to see her friends as she explained but there was more to her outings. Mellissa would sleep throughout the day and night; she would never run out of sleep. Meme too was enjoying the epitome of freedom; immediately after breakfast she would leave the house to join her peers. She would play all day and stay outdoors till late; at times Sisi, on her way home would see her and drag her home. Sometimes I had to look for her. Even worse, at times we would all panic when we could not find her. Then, she would be brought home by one of her friends' elder siblings.

The holiday came to an end and schools opened. I was not going to school as I awaited my 'O' level exam results. But because I had to take Meme and Mimi to school, we all had to wake up early. Sisi had to prepare their lunch boxes, uniforms and help with school preparations which included workbooks. It can be safely concluded that Mellissa was the lazy one; she loathed the walks from town to and from school. She would ask me to carry her on the back. I never agreed because if anyone had to be carried it had to be Mimi. Mellissa would then resolve to being sulky and irritable. We had warmed up to each other over the years. After supper we would sit in the dining room and engaged in conversations.

"The money Uncle Nongai had left me is finished guys and tomorrow you need to go to school," I said teasing. Meme was undoubtedly pleased to hear that and surprisingly so was Mimi.

"It's okay *Bhudhi*[35] Mutsva. We'll go to school when mama and daddy have returned," said Mimi unbothered.

"Good news could never be better. So tomorrow we don't have to wake up at the crack of dawn," responded Meme.

Whilst we were sitting and chatting the electricity went off. Before I could tell them, I was pulling their legs, Sisi immediately ushered them to their bedroom. With the lights off, it got boring with no television to watch nor radio to listen to.

The next morning when I woke up, Sisi was up and the girls were still sleeping. I told her I was merely joking and asked her to wake them up and prepare them for school.

As she woke them up, I could hear them remonstrating. I went to join them, so I could explain myself and convince them to prepare for school. Mimi was even

---

[35] Brother

crying complaining of how much her tummy was hurting her; she even ran to the toilet. How she had thought of that plan left us astounded. Upon her return, she went straight back to bed and the more she tried convincing us she was telling the truth, the more hilarious it became. We laughed so much at her until she busted out of the room again headed to the bathroom. Sisi followed her and saw as she attempted vomiting but nothing came out. Unaware if this was just still a trick or if she was seriously ill, Sisi and I became confused. Meme blatantly refused to go to school seeing the way Mimi displayed being sick. We eventually agreed that they would stay at home with the hope that Mimi would be well the following day.

The day passed, Mimi did not leave the house, she kept on passing diarrhoea and she vomited all she had eaten. Unaware of the cause of her sudden stomach bug, I became unsettled. This was unlike Mimi. If it were a mere excuse for her to abscond attending school, she would have left the house immediately after breakfast to play outside as usual. Her reluctance to leave the house and the continuation of her abdominal pain, diarrhoea and eventually vomiting became alarming.

Dzivarasekwa did not have any prominent bushes; I would have immediately searched for some remedy for my little sister. Misery veiled the house as we all became distressed by Mimi's sudden illness.

I then remembered the gumtree plantation that was along the road that headed towards the informal settlements. Gumtrees grow in a manner that reduces chances of growth of any other species through its expansive and wide spreading roots. The only exception is one tenacious tree species called *Mukina*[36] or *Musiringa.* It managed to thrive and grow amidst the plantation as a result of its reseeding proneness and easy naturalization. I had learnt of this tree's agriculture profile and at home I had often heard people's conversation about how its leaves aided with resolving diarrhoea.

I went to the plantation and was lucky to locate a Mukina tree close to the edges of the plantation. Quickly, I pruned a handful of leaves through the barbed wire fence. Ignoring the minor mishap of a few cuts on my arm, I clasped the leaves and ran back home. Having never used these tree leaves before I did not know with certainty if what I intended to do would work. If not helpful, I just hoped it would not aggravate her state. As I had heard it helped others so it would help Mimi get better too!

I got home and found Sisi waiting for me, a pot with boiling water was already on the stove as we had both agreed to give it a try. Sisi washed the leaves and threw them into the boiling water. After immersing the leaves in the water for long enough, she sieved the green coloured water into a cup. It took patience and intense negotiation to get Mimi to drink the concoction. At 16:00 she was done drinking a cup full and she retired to sleep. We did not eat much at supper as we were all troubled. Mimi did not wake up to join us for super; Meme and Sisi went to check on her. Somnolent, I slept while sitting on the sofa in the living room.

"Bhudhi Mutsva, Bhudhi Mutsva," called out Meme as she woke me up.

To my surprise it was barely 2 am. I realised I had

---

[36] the Melia Azedarach tree

slept on the sofa, which irked aunty Maggie so much. Grateful for her not having witnessed it, I woke up and immediately stood up. Meme pulled my hand towards her bedroom.

"Sisi is calling you to come and see."

I reeled to her pull. I was relieved to see Mimi sitting on the bed. "Mimi, are you okay," I asked going to sit next to her placing my hand around her shoulder.

Non-verbally she responded, with a smirk and Nodded.

"She is okay. She hasn't vomited or gone to the toilet since drinking that cup of medication. I called for you because I heard movements outside and I saw lights flashing," responded Sisi directing my focus to the window where there was light flushing from outside.

There seemed to be movement accompanied by incoherent chatter. There were people roaming about the yard. They were eventually going to attempt to get into the house. At this hour, it could only mean one thing.

7 Misunderstood

By the time when the door was unlocked, we had hidden Meme and Mimi in the wardrobe. This was my time to shine. Above all, this was the prime reason why Uncle Nongai had brought me before departing. I had my catapult ready to directly hit the eye of the invader or at least the forehead, a knife for control in case the stone did not frighten them enough. I however, had no intention to cause terminal harm to anyone.

Sisi waited in the bathroom with the door closed enough for her safety and for her to be able to hear what was happening. She also had a whistle ready. In the event that I succumbed at the hand of the invaders, she would blow it as a call out for help from the neighbours. To bolster our plan Meme had a phone, at the sound of the whistle, she would call the police and notify them of a robbery taking place. The door unlocked with close to no struggling effort. It was Uncle Nongai and mainini whom had returned home. Upon hearing the voice of their parents, immediately they hasted out of the wardrobe, opened the bedroom door and ran towards their parents. After embracing them into their arms, Uncle Nongai and mainini sat down and we exchanged greetings. It was late to have ongoing conversations so at once Uncle No dismissed us all to go and sleep. Mimi still looked withdrawn and insisted on sharing her parent's bed. I looked forward to seeing her looking better the following day.

I had barely slept for three hours when I woke to culinary banging noises in the kitchen. Mainini was speaking at the top of her voice. I wondered what could have gone wrong so early and so soon after just returning from a vacation. Everyone seemed to have woken up, I hesitated to get into the kitchen and greet her but I could not stay in my bedroom as if I had something to hide or was guilty.

As I walked to the kitchen my eyes caught sight of Meme. She had her whole focus deep into her cereal, dressed up and ready for school with her lunchbox ready right next to her bowl of cereal. She looked discontented; I would have expected her to be in delight as she was no longer going to use public transport. Mimi was not in the kitchen. Imaginably, she was still feeling under the weather. Sisi was busy on the sink. I could not exactly tell what she was busy washing. Aunty Maggie was busy up and down, closing and opening every single drawer of the cupboards. Uncle No was not in the picture, perhaps he was still resting. "*Mamukasei,*"[37] I said as I entered into the kitchen with my morning greetings. I only got Mainini's attention. Meme and Sisi seemed not to notice my presence or hear my greeting.

---

[37] Goodmorning

Aunty Maggie stood and faced me with her right hand in which she was holding a dish towel resting on her waist.
"Mimi *akatanga kurwara rinhi nhai Mutsva*?"[38]

I was not expecting to be greeted back that way. With the look of fury on her face, I immediately realised that I was setting off for a trip in the furnace.

"Yesterday, mainini. She woke up complaining of a tummy ache. She had a running tummy and she was vomiting."

"So, tell me, what stopped you from taking her to the hospital?"

I had no idea of how to answer her question. To be honest, I thought Mimi would recover without needing hospital care and when all this happened. We were caught unaware naturally. We got confused to even think of the hospital. In all the four years I had stayed in Harare, I had never been to any hospital or clinic as there had been no reason for me to do so. Not that I would not have known where to find a health care centre, I used to see a number of them along the roads especially the big Parirenyatwa Group of hospitals which was close to where my school was. I remained silent and she continued,

"And you thought to make a doctor out of your sorry self, trying your ideas on my daughter. This is pathetic, what about calling us the parents if you did not know what to do?"

"I'm sorry mainini," I said filled with guilt. If anything, she was justified to be upset. We had not dealt with this in the best way as much as we had thought or rather as much as I had thought.

---

[38] When did Mimi fall ill Mutsva?

"I don't know. Either you're dumb or you're selfish and you don't care. I don't know, *hambeno handizive*[39]. I took you in with love Mutsva *heee*? I treated you as my own but this is how you decide to watch over my child, gambling with her life? As I am alive *kudai*[40]. What more if I'm dead? I swear with what you have shown me *ukasaroya iwe uchaba*[41]", she concluded with tears streaming down her face whilst looking at me. She threw the dish towel onto the table where Meme was just poking into her cereal and walked towards me. With the back of her left hand, she pushed me aside and passed by. She went to her bedroom where we could all hear her mourn.

Uncle Nongai came into the kitchen from outside, I gathered he had woken up earlier and he was only coming back. He was already dressed up, he exchanged morning greetings with everyone and he turned down Sisi's offer to serve him with breakfast. He did not say much but I could tell how he was also disappointed and not pleased with me. He went to his bedroom and within a few minutes he came out holding his briefcase.

"Meme, you should have been done already. If you don't want to eat, cover your plate and stop playing with food. Take your bag; let's go," he said as he headed towards the door and mainini walked behind him quietly with swollen and reddened eyes.

"Bye-bye," whispered Meme to Sisi and I as she took her lunch box and grabbed her bag following her parents. She was out of the door before we could even say bye to her too. I could not imagine how tense the

---

[39] I don't know

[40] as is

[41] if you will not become a witch, you will become a thief

environment would be in the car. I felt sorry for Meme. She had to endure the drive all alone.

I left the kitchen to go and check on Mimi; she was not on the bed. Immediately I went to ask Sisi if perhaps she knew about Mimi's whereabouts and she told me that she had a minor convulsion just before dawn and a fever which made mainini and Uncle Nongai drive her immediately to the hospital. She had been admitted for continued care and observation. That is where Uncle No had been coming from and also where mainini was going. She was not going to work but to the hospital to spend the day on her daughter's bedside.

If I could, I would have packed my bags and left right away for home. Unfortunately, I had to wait until my 'O' level exams results were published. I would go home and share them with my parents then come back again to Dzivarasekwa, the only place I had to stay while going to school. The anger, disengagement and misunderstanding that occupied the house created a hostile environment, staying anywhere had never been this unpleasant.

It was on a Thursday at around four, early in the morning. We woke up to noise of cries, screams and crowds engaging in conversations, also unusual hooting by cars. As I remained in my room, I heard Uncle Nongai and mainini wake up and without even a sound of splashing water from the bathroom they left the house. Immediately after their exit and locking of the door, Sisi came knocking on my door. Sisi and I were officially a tag-team, over the four years we had grown to have an understanding of each other and nobly became friends; we engaged in conversations about everything. She entered my room and did not close the door lest she had to race back to her room soon as her bosses returned. As soon as she sat on the chair next to my study desk, Meme followed. She sat on my bed, leaning on the wall and covered herself with my throw over blanket.

"Where is this noise coming from; what do you suppose is going on?"

"I wish I knew; you have many friends around here Meme and you Sisi. Why don't you call them to ask?"

"Okay but who?" asked Sisi with great curiosity.

"Call Chioniso," Meme suggested. Chioniso was Sisi's friend who also worked in one of the houses in our neighbourhood.

"Good, yeah let me call her… Hi Chioniso, can you hear the noise from outside in the road?"

Expectantly Meme and I looked at Sisi as she engaged in a conversation with her friend. We wanted to know what they were talking about as Sisi's face was showing vagueness. She continued,

"Mmm, I see. Mmm mmm true eish but eish it doesn't make sense still but well what can we say? I can imagine okay thank you bye *sha.*[42]"

"What did she say," Meme and I chorused as soon as Sisi got off the phone. She clearly knew something now. Maybe not the whole detail but a little bit of something.

"It's sad. Apparently, there is the Doves funeral parlour car which she just saw driving by and it looked as if it had a coffin. When she also called Rudo, Rudo said the coffin was the size for a child."

Before we could invest more in the discussion, we then heard Uncle Nongai and mainini opening the gate. Immediately, Meme jumped off my bed and ran to her room and so did Sisi. Ever since Mimi's admission into

---

[42] Shortcut for 'shamwari' which means friend

the hospital there was just too much distrust. It felt as if it was getting worse. Nothing was happening to improve the atmosphere. As I lay on my bed, I could hear all of Aunty Maggie and Uncle Nongai's movements. I did not pay attention to their conversation. I knew they would be discussing what had happened. My thoughts were drawn to wondering how worse the situation would be if Mimi were to pass on.

Many times, I had resolved to using plant remedies to assist the unwell but none of them had made it to healing and living longer. Mainini was right I should have not made a doctor out of my sorry self. I should have learnt my lesson with my first attempt at Gogo's wound and not relied on herbal remedies. How stupid I had been. Careless and unrealistic. Indeed, I needed someone, just one person to confront me and mainini had been brave enough. If anything, I should have been grateful that she did. I had to stop my delusional belief of plants being natural remedies for illness. I swore to myself with tears streaming down the side of my eyeballs to my ears, to never pluck out a plant, leaf, bark or anything with the intention to heal any unwellness. Never again would the bush be my sanctuary.

I was awoken by Meme's knock on my door.

"Bhudhi Mutsva Daddy is calling for you."

At once I jumped out of bed and went to the sitting room where I found him together with mainini and Sisi[43] sitting on the sofa. Meme went to sit next to Sisi and Uncle Nongai was sitting on his singular sofa. The only space available was on the double seat sofa that mainini was sitting on. I was not brave enough to seat next to her. I

---

[43] Sister

took a chair from the kitchen and brought it into the sitting room. I sat next to the sofa Sisi and Meme were sharing and facing Uncle No directly. I had never been to an interview or board room for a presentation but rest assured the room would suit the atmosphere. Soon as I sat down Uncle Nongai looked at me.

"Are you now deaf?"

It does not rain but it pours. I did not know what he was on about so I did not know how to respond to him. I kept quiet and continued looking at him to reassure him that I was not ignoring him but I did not know what he was talking about.

"You even have the audacity to look straight into my eyes. So much disrespect, heeeee? 10 minutes calling you, your age sleeping as if you are dead heee?"

"*Uyu adzika midzi*[44], the disrespect he is showing Lately I wonder. *Anoita zvemusoro wake zvake*[45]," responded mainini loudly and fuelling up Uncle Nongai's rage. She spoke with great fury. The way she was moving her hands, if I had gone to seat next to her, I would surely had been double clapped.

"Mutsva, I don't know what to say," Uncle Nongai looked at me with ridicule, nodding his head in disappointment. "I called you all to tell you that *PaMlambo* a child has passed on. Apparently, she had cholera, it's sad very young. The story is very unclear if it was just cholera or other ailments contributed to her demise. The news also has been reporting of a cholera and typhoid outbreak…"

"If my child dies Mutsva. If she just, she just, just, just.

---

[44] he has become unruly

[45] He does as he pleases

Mmm *Ngozi yangu unoiona iwe itai henyu.*[46]"

"But I'm not done talking can you allow me to finish," said Uncle Nongai frustrated at mainini for interrupting him.

"Nongai, Nongai, this is on you too, you and your family *mese*[47]."

Mainini was not taking any of this well. I had made peace with my wrongs but hearing her speak to Uncle Nongai that way broke my heart. I hated being the reason to break their marriage. That would haunt me.

"Maggie, calm down Mimi is recovering. So Sisi, please I would like to ask you to go over to the Mlambos and assist them where they need an extra hand. I unfortunately, can't be of much help. I am going to work and *Mai M*[48] will be spending the day with Mimi watching to her needs at the hospital. Meme you will join your mother. And Mutsva tomorrow, I've arranged for you to take the 6 o'clock Kukura Kurerwa bus. I need you to take a parcel for me home. So today you make preparations for the journey."

We all agreed. It was only Sisi, Meme and I who were in the dark and had not much of a choice really. News of me being sent back home was of great relief as I had been longing to escape how horrid Harare had become for me. I just needed to have my peace restored. Haplessly, I still had controversy waiting for me at home, the dilemma of having to choose one of my two brothers.

---

[46] you will see my wrath, continue as you are doing and you shall see

[47] All of you

[48] Mother of M

8 Quest of Happiness

Going back home and explaining what had happened in Harare had not affected Baba and his brother's relationship. They had continued having frequent telephonic conversation and baba would share with us everything they would have talked about. Mama, on the other hand, had developed an instant hatred for mainini. Whenever Baba was on the phone with Uncle Nongai, she would wave her hand, a sign to show that if they ask for her, Baba should tell them of her absence. I had tried to justify to her that I understood the reason why mainini had gotten angry to the point of saying such harsh words. However, to her defence mama had exclaimed that she had no right to curse me. I wished I had not told them everything. I only did so with the intention for them to understand the whole picture; I suppose I should have known better.

I expected the estrangement between Chamuka and Maneta naturally to still be persisting. To my surprise, they came to pay me a visit together. I identified their voices, as I was behind the kitchen fixing the dish drying platform, *dara*[49]. Mama kept on complaining that her plates were falling off from it as it had loosened due to the heavy monsoon rains. They exchanged greetings with mama as it was just after lunch and she was relaxing on the reed mat under the mango tree.

"Maneta so nice to see you. It's been long without seeing the both of you. I'd have been happier if you'd come with my grand-child." She laughed. "I'm so happy for you, congratulations, how are they doing at home?"

Mama had asked something that could brew tension instantly. However, they both seemed relaxed and Maneta freely continued with the conversation.

"Hahaha. Wisdom and his mother they are alright thank you. We will pay you a visit together soon."

"Aaah an English name! hehehe *muruda tione makafunda here*[50]?

Mama made a loud laugh and I heard her clap her hands in excitement. What was mind blowing was hearing Maneta and Chamuka joining in to share with her the moment. I was finally at home, the kind of home I knew to have been looking forward to going; a home with people whom I valued most and seeing them in good cheer fulfilled me. Mama continued to direct them to where I was.

As they headed towards me, they were mumbling. I concluded that they were avoiding their conversation being heard. I was not surprised this was so usual of them, being in cahoots.

---

49 dish drying platform

50 you want us to see that you are educated

I was happy to see them. We hung around behind the kitchen for a while as I finished my task.

We walked Maneta home first because he was now a family man and had to return home on time. On the other hand, when I was walking Chamuka home he was unusually distant and seemed uncomfortable with me. There was no reason for him to be estranged with me, so immediately I confronted him.

"Chamuka, is there something that you would like us to discuss?"

"No nothing, we good why?"

"You just don't seem to be yourself. This I would expect with Maneta being around, but surprisingly you seemed better in his presence and now he has left you seem off."

"No, brotherhood is important. We sorted out our differences so we are good."

"Oh okay, so what is it?"

"Nothing. Relax. Nothing is wrong. Stop overthinking man. Okay, I will see you later. I'm going to pass by the store so ok I'll see you tomorrow."

"It's fine I can come with you; mama knows I went out with you so yeah let's go."

"No, this is a one-man mission. I'll see you tomorrow."

At once, he quickly set off in the opposite direction of his home; I could not even delay or follow him. What was Chamuka hiding from me? I was going to find out soon enough; he was the clumsiest with secrets, when he got a little excited, he would let loose.

Days passed; I had not found an opportunity to meet Maneta or Chamuka. Maneta was preferably familiar with farming, after failing his 'O' Levels he pursued being a commercial farmer. That was how he earned a living and provided for his family, to his advantage his family owned a vast piece of land and his father gave him a generous portion. He was good at what he did, he yielded gruesome heaps of harvest. The pecks of adulting, I could barely see Maneta as he was forever busy on his land.

Chamuka was the socialite of us all. Not much of a hard worker, he preferred the easier way of surviving. He too did not pass his 'O' level and he did not have any intentions of going back to school and try again. He set off on the use of his family's cow drawn cart as his source of income, through transporting people, offering to carry parcels or even firewood anything that required transportation. He was the main source of transport in our village. His business was growing, he bought his own three carts and a remarkable herd of cattle. In the times of sowing, farmers would hire his cows for ploughing which saw him having an additional source of income. He too obtained a piece of land to cultivate on from his father. To maximize his profits, he also bought a plough. He would use it to cultivate his land and some farmers would also hire it. Chamuka was a jack of all trades and was arguably the wealthiest of the three of us. Considering that he had no responsibilities, all his profits went to expanding his work.

I was proud of both of my brothers. However, I could not help but reflect; it seemed my life was lagging behind ever since I had to repeat my grade seven. Even so, their lifestyle could never be for me; I had become drawn to the city lifestyle. I had gained exposure from travelling which had greatly impacted my perspective on life. There were opportunities that lay beyond my village that I aspired and yearned for. I did not want just to be comfortable but I wanted the finest luxury's that the world could offer as I had witnessed. School was not the way of life for all of us but it was my path and I was willing to walk the long journey and own my path. A little patience, determination and more of hard work was what I needed to dwell on.

Miriro would grace my loneliness with her visits. She would accompany me to get water from the well by the river. A full drum would give sufficient water for a day or two. In order to fill it up I had to do four trips. Miriro would accompany me on all of the four trips, leaving four full extra water buckets in mama's kitchen. I would push the wheelbarrow containing three twenty- litre water bottles and she would carry on her head one water bucket. Mama had grown fond of her; she called her a daughter she would have loved to have. Miriro was not only doing this because I was around, even in my absence she would pay visits and help mama with cleaning or giving her any assistance she needed. She would leave water buckets filled up with water for mama's use.

I felt she was doing too much for us and yet I did not do anything for her in return. So, I offered to get her firewood from the forest as I was certain she needed it at home. She rejected my offer saying they had found a regular supplier who delivered firewood to their home and she was only repaying the kindness we had initially shown her.

A couple of weeks passed without seeing Maneta and Chamuka so I decided to pay Maneta a visit. Fortunately, I found *Baba* Wisdom sitting on a stool and he was sewing a pair of his shoes and his child was crawling around him. "For once, you're not toiling," I said approaching him.

"Hahaha I'm a family man, what would you expect," said my friend as he stood up to greet me.

Maneta was not just a family man but a happy family man. He offered me a seat on his stool and he sat on the reed mat that lay next to his stool. I assumed Chamuka's sister, *Mai* Wisdom had been seating on it and just left it there.

"What have you been up to Mutsva? Don't hesitate to pay a visit when you get bored. I will never stop working if no one draws me out of the field. Often Rugare has to call me back home otherwise I live in the field."

"I'll definitely remember that next time I find myself idle. I've been having some company off late."

Rugare came to greet me and she offered me food which I refused as I honestly had no appetite. I had an important matter to discuss with my friend. It was about Miriro. At first, I thought it was my mother's praises and emphasis on how much an impressive girl she was that was putting ideas in my head so I ignored it, until I realised how low my mood would be whenever she did not pay a visit. Nothing would interest me, not even food. I was addicted to her presence. I had always liked Miriro as she had a noble character, the same way I had liked Meme, Mimi, Matipa as well as Chamuka's sisters. But I had never felt the need of their company. I still knew not where she stayed. Perhaps that was a bit ignorant of me but I had never thought that I would grow to the point of having a constant longing for her company. I had never had an issue with being a loner. This was beyond liking; I had fallen in love with her.

Once Rugare left holding Wisdom in her hands, Maneta continued, "So who has been keeping you company, yeah it was high time my friend."

Maneta's smile reassured me, so I began. "I know nothing about love and you do, so I want to know. How do you know if it's love or just?"

"It's different my friend to tell you the truth. It's just something that you feel, I don't even know how to explain it. Okay, I met Rugare that time when we'd paid Chamu visits I just liked her. But the few minutes of conversations we would have made me grow fond of her. At times my aim would be going to just check on Rugare, when I'd visit and find that he is not around, you know Chamuka is always everywhere I would maximize the time and have conversations with her. We just grew to be good company for each other. On paying a visit to their home sometimes I wouldn't find her home and that disappointment my friend would cut deep, everything even Chamuka himself would annoy the life out of me."

He was laughing. The joy and happiness he showed on reminiscing was ridiculous. Love can make people go mad, but I could relate to exactly how he felt because I also felt that towards Miriro. At least he could steal time to go and see her when he missed her but what about me? I could never do that because I did not know where to find her. I was clueless about this love business. My brothers were winning and I the city boy still had a long way to go.

Maneta then continued, "Plus love in secrecy is amusing. I think the danger of avoiding being caught makes it interesting, you do all you can to enjoy each other in the little time you have together. Love is fulfilling I tell you. Enough about me, you seem unsettled what's up?"

"I'm not sure but I came here with an issue which I would like to discuss with you. There's a girl that I like but I don't really know if I like her as much as you like Rugare.

We've spent so much time together and we enjoy each other's company that it frustrates the life out of me when I don't get to see her."

"We can never love the same way,"
responded Maneta, trying to encourage me.
"The way I or Chamu or you love or can be loved can never be the same."

I had not heard of any news with regards to Chamu being in love. As his best friend I was offended to be unaware. Perhaps our friendship was ruined by the different ways of life we had grown to lead. I was beginning to feel excluded from our friendship. Just when I was glad that our trio was back in union. Overly I was curious to know, "Chamu? in love, who got through that cracknut?"

"Aaah you don't know? I thought he'd have told you. What were you talking about after I left?"

"Nothing much he was in a hurry to do his errands, just tell me."

"Oh, I see; he's been busy lately. He says he wants to be well established before marrying as he isn't impulsive and naïve as some of us. He wants to be ready before marrying."

"Chamu, marrying? I don't believe you."

"At first she made him forgive me and talk to me. So, we restored our friendship. All of a sudden, he became a jovial fellow. I thought it was just his business growing well until I realised that he was delivering firewood to this girl's house on a regular basis. I'm telling you, that girl you know her. She would come over to your house and help mama that's how I got to know her. Chamu would wait for her and when she'd leave your home they'd meet."

I could hardly come to terms with what Maneta had told me, Miriro and Chamu. I could blame them for betraying me but I had never confessed my feelings to Miriro nor did I own her. One could easily fall in love with her after getting to spend time with her. I avoided having any further conversation with Maneta and with a heavy heart I left for home. I felt blue, down in the dumps.

Withdrawn into my shell, I went straight to my room and slept off my disappointment. A knock on my door woke me up. It was mama. When she needed a friend, she made it a point to bore me with the village drama. I entertained her because what else could I do. However, with the way I was, I could not be the best company for her so half-heartedly and with guilt I ignored her call for me to open the door for her. I wanted to sleep for forever or perhaps waking up to a realization that it had been a nightmare.

I woke up to another loud call of my name echoing from the kitchen. It was time for supper. If it were up to me, I would have skipped it because of the awful state I was in but my parents would not accept such a behaviour. It would come across as disrespect after all Baba had to go through to source the food and for Mama to prepare it. All I was expected to do was join them and enjoy their effort. Supper in my home was a family session where we talked, joked and laughed.

As expected, I joined my parents for supper. Immediately after clearing up the plates, Uncle Nongai called baba. Whatever news he received brightened his face. I waited impatiently for Baba to drop the call that we may pray and disperse for sleep. As much as I figured my name being overwhelmingly involved in their conversation, I was sincerely uninterested in hearing about it. Zealously, after dropping the call baba could not wait to share with us what Uncle No had told him.

"Nongai just shared Mutsva's results with me, well done my son."

My mother stood up with the speed of lightning from the reed mat, jumping up and down in celebratory mode on alternate feet. She did a whirlwind dance, ululating.

I smiled at the realization of how proud I had made them. I loved and lived to impress my parents. They had gone above and beyond for me; they had done everything possible to give me the best upbringing. My heartbreak clouded me from entirely celebrating my achievement. After praying, in thanksgiving mama singularly prayed for my achievement and blessed my return to Harare. We had not discussed the way forward but from her prayer I knew I was going to be on my way to Dzivarasekwa sooner than I had thought.

I did not want to go back to stay with mainini. It had been awkward enough when I left. I knew when I left her house that I would have to return at some point. The reality of the time being now distressed me. I was already dispirited; I could not imagine the sight of Miriro and Chamu being together. The only two homes I had grown to know were Nyamhere village and at mainini's in Dzivarasekwa and yet I did not wish to be at either of them. I slept trying to figure out if I was cursed or rather a lost cause because my happiness was never definite.

9 The Squad

Uncle Nongai as usual picked me up from Harare's Mbare bus terminus. On our way home he was pre-occupied with excitement from the grades of excellence I had attained. After graciously congratulating me, we conversed as if I had left all in good order.

On the second day after my return, I had the opportunity to sit down and talk with mainini. She sincerely emphasized on how she had impulsively acted out of anger and did not mean many of the words she had said towards me. I held no grudge against her because in all honesty, I was in the wrong and I entirely took the blame for the tension between mama and mainini. I honoured her invitation of peace and have things work in my favour. Thankfully, being back at Dzivarasekwa turned out not to be as bad as I had presumed.

A week before going back to school, baba sold two of the Guernsey's from his herd and sent money to Uncle Nongai. It was his contribution to my school tuition. He had figured that to minimize spending most of my time wayfaring to and from school through town I had to be enrolled in boarding school. Uncle Nongai welcomed and agreed to this suggestion as he reckoned that studying Advanced Level would be more intense as compared to Ordinary Level. I could be wrong but knowing my mother, this was a plan orchestrated by her. She had sworn to never let me live in Dzivarasekwa again.

I had never thought I would enrol in boarding school as it seemed an option for the wealthy elites only. As unexpected as it was, I gladly welcomed the suggestion. I wanted to maintain the good relations I had restored with Uncle Nongai and mainini; not being in their space seemed to be an ideal way to maintain the reconciliation. Moreover, I needed to make a couple of new friends and learn the way of life in the city. I appreciated my background. It had moulded me into who I was but it was time for me to grow beyond that. I needed to learn, understand and live both the rural and the uptown life.

Seemingly, there was not much left for me in Nyamhere except for my parents. I felt betrayed and hollow knowing that what I had ascertained to provide me with happiness had been snatched away from me by my own brother. Just the sheer thought of it brought my blood hot, into a boiling rage. Nyamhere was definitely not what I needed and I could not wait to immerse and lose myself in the new challenge, my academics and the boarding school environment.

Admission into boarding school was easy because I was an old boy with pleasing grades. The headmaster took me in without hesitation. As seniors we had the privilege of having single room dormitories. I appreciated having my own space. Tawanda was my neighbour, he was nicknamed 'Lowe' after one of the greatest Zimbabwean swimmer 'David Lowe' because he swam like a sailfish. He occupied the room next to mine. He was the only one I managed to click with as we both attended the mathematics class and sat on the same table in the dining hall. My math prowess encouraged our friendship because I would assist him whenever he struggled, which were countless times.

Whenever Lowe had a swimming competition, he would invite me to come along and I would gladly do to support him. The extent of feeling that traversed the school bus, filled with fervent athletes plugged with triumphant descants was contagious. The athletes group had a strong union; they supported each other in order to uphold the winning name of the school. Lowe would go to every sports competition to support, as he knew most of the fellow athletes. He would invite me to come along and that is how I got to engage with more individuals and got more friends. As I never had been the one to be competitive in sports, only the jack of academics, I got instigated to become a vibrant support comrade. I did not just know every song, I knew how to whistle, dance and also drum to them. Singing was second nature when you were a boarder; we would sing beyond the sports bus trips and sports fields. This was our sole entertainment. This got to be my new way of life and I took in every moment of it.

On returning to the dormitories from the sports events, we would gather in an individual's room where the feasting mode of celebration would be actuated. Pablo one of Lowe's friends was the chief of smuggling hence his nickname. Pablo would source alcohol and space cookies and hid them in Lowe's room; obviously it was my best friend's room so I joined in the party and would pay Pablo the fee due to him. They were great evenings; happiness would fill the room and those moments made it seem as if nothing would ever go wrong in life. We progressed with singing, our nonsense chatter, mocked the teachers, our peers and even teased each other's dressing, girlfriends; anything, you name it, everything was for the taking and fun was the order of the night. I suppose we would get drunk but there was no harm in having the good time.

I had mastered the art of balancing my studies and allowing myself to have fun. I grew comfortable with being in a space of only men such that I would struggle to interact with the girls. I would resolve to heedlessly loiter around alone after sports impatiently anticipating the departure of the school bus.

On one swimming event, as we sat on the top terraces five girls came to sit on the lower terrace because the upper seats had been taken by other patrons. When supporting swimming, we did not sing as much as we did at the ball games. The moment they saw the girls; my company became unsteady. Jimmalo started laughing and Mugadza was rubbing his hands, smiling looking at me and Pablo. I was the least they would expect to initiate a conversation with the girls so I left the honours to Pablo who was sitting on my right. I patted him on the back and he resolutely stood and took a few steps down to approach the girls.

Pablo had a gift. He had the girls giggling and laughing within a few minutes. Seeing that he was winning, the three of us bet on the girl we thought he would pick of the five. As we were talking, he turned his head towards us and with a smile he lifted his thumb. Surprisingly, the girl I had bet he would take began climbing up the terraces. She was obviously coming to us. Avoiding making a fool out of myself by getting involved I redirected my focus to the pool, my eyes checking for Lowe, after all we were here to support him. He was sitting on the competitor's terraces and I caught him looking our direction so I waved at him. In response, with a big smile as if he wanted to laugh, he gestured with his hands; I figured he was asking what was going on, I did not know too so I threw both my hands in the air to show him that I had no idea what was happening and that was the truth.

"Hey," she said standing directly in front of me in such a way that I could not ignore her.

With everything in me, I calmly turned towards her with a polite smile and extended my hand, "Hey, hey, how is it?"

"I'm good, so Mutsva right?"

"Yes, correct. I am," I scoffed because I wanted to laugh. Lowe was still looking our direction. How could Jimmalo and Mugadza throw me under the bus? They continued conversing as if they did not see what was happening.

"It's alright, uhm what is his name?" she said pointing at Pablo.

So, who told her about me if she did not know the first guy to approach her and her friends? I thought to myself. I did not ask her lest I would have been regarded as rude.

"Oh, that's Pablo and I might as well introduce them all to you, the light one on my left is Jimmalo and the chap sitting next to him is Mugadza."

"Nice meeting you guys," she said smiling.

Confidently, she extended her hand towards them greeting Mugadza first then Jimmalo who then opened up space between him and I for her and offered her a seat. I had not supposed she had come to stay so I had not thought of offering her a seat and also as usual I had no idea how to socialise in general but thank God for charmer boy Jimmalo.

"Thank you, I'm Runyararo but you can call me Runya; your friend what's his name again?"

"Pablo," I responded quickly because I wanted her to finish what she had come for and go as I was getting uncomfortable with her presence.

"Yes, right Pablo. So, he came to us and said he was sent by you to ask me if I could be kind enough and allow you to talk to me, so I thought to be nicer and came up here."

"Me," I asked her surprised.

"Yes, he said Mutsva," she said looking at me with her back on Jimmalo who was quietly laughing. He even fell on Mugadza's legs; they were both having the best laugh. I could not believe Pablo. I got tongue tied. To my rescue Mugadza joined in our conversation.

"Oh yeah, hey Runyararo you know what happened when Mutsva saw you, he said you looked like someone he knows but he wasn't sure. I suppose Pablo being curious as always, he took the chance to confirm by telling you Mutsva wanted to talk to you, you know."

"I see. So do you know me?"

"This is embarrassing but no I guess you just look alike. But nice to meet you. So, are you coming to support a schoolmate or a friend?"

"No, we just came to see. No one we know is participating. And you guys?"

"We're here to cheer for our boy."

"Oh nice. So, is he winning?"

"So far so good. He has promising points. We waiting for the quarter finals."

"*Runyararo! Let's go.*"

"All the best to him hey; I got to go; my friend is calling me."

"Already, why so quick? Are they bored? Perhaps we should ask them to all come up," I said lying through my teeth, yet I was relieved.

"No, it's okay we didn't intend to be here for long, but nice seeing you once again I hope to see you around soon."

"Definitely. We are always around." Immediately, I stood up and helped her stand up too. She waved to the boys and Jimmalo signalled to me with his hands that I should walk her down to where her friends were calling her so I did but not too close to where her friends were lest my performance blew off.

As I climbed up the terraces back to the laughing hyenas with another one behind me, the greatest culprit Pablo, I could not help but blurt out all the laughter I was also concealing.

"I saw you; I saw you zhhhh[51]! Welcome to the game! So how was it," Pablo said as he was approaching us.

"What can I say, I was born a natural team player, the game is on," I said feeling triumphant.

"Did you get the cell phone number," asked Pablo.

"How? This one he didn't have the stamina; we had to help, chipping in and creating a lie to see him through otherwise he was going to jump off this terrace," Jimmalo sarcastically responded whilst theatrically chocking on laughter.

---

[51] Sound students make when excited

"Get away, I had the stamina but I did not have time, you cannot just hop into asking for that. Those are sensitive matters."

The gang just broke into laughter and I knew that I would never hear the end of that matter. I would be teased about this day forever. They laughed at me that we forgot about Lowe's last race.

Immediately after he finished, he came running up to join us.

The following term when we returned from the second term holiday there were not as many sports activities on the school calendar. I got occupied with my studies, I had not forgotten the reason why I had been avoiding to go back home. I chose to redirect my focus towards things that did not discourage me nor overwhelm me with negativity and these were my academics and my life at Dub. The headmaster had often checked in with me to ensure that I had not let the company of my friends get in the way of my academic excellence. I never lost focus on the main objective, academic excellence. There was no going back, I had to make it, if anything, I owed my parents that honour.

In A Level, it was an encouraged tradition to attend academic seminars, as they provided all the A Level student's with sufficient exposure and know how on the best way to answer examination questions through the facilitated discussions we engaged in. I was given the opportunity to present at the first Mathematics seminar of the year that was being hosted at our school. As expected, I made a good impression of our math department and after the seminar had ended as we were meeting and greeting, I felt a pat on my back.

"Your presentation was spot on, you made it look as if math is easy."

I took it as a compliment. I knew if there was anything I did effortlessly and enjoyed, it was calculating maths. I turned to see who it was. Matipa! She looked so beautiful I could never have thought of her to grow and look any different or perhaps it was because I had not seen her for close to three years. In the spur of the moment, I hugged her with excitement. We had a conversation as if it were only the two of us around; completely ignoring the swarm of intellects conversing around us.

After our reconciliation, Matipa and I kept on communicating and we often met at the seminars. She knew as well as understood me better. The fact that I could be myself with her as much as she could also be herself gleaned chemistry between the two of us. Before we even had gotten into a relationship my squad had already officiated us. 'How is your girlfriend?' had become the famous question I had to answer. Having a relationship with Matipa covered up my shortfall of socializing with girls. I needed not try to prove my manliness to the squad anymore. I never got to be mocked about what happened with Runyararo. Actually, looking at it perhaps I was just selectively social and not completely unable to socialise with girls.

It had been two years since I had been back home. Being a boarder played a significant role to that. Spending time with Lowe, Pablo, Jimmalo and Mugadza and engaging in conversations with many of my peers enlightened me to a different life dimension which, I would not have had if I had not continued with my studies nor studied in the capital city. Matipa had been advised by her brother to apply for the presidential scholarships so that she could attain funding to study abroad, if possible, even in Botswana, since he had already established himself and his family there. When she shared the idea with me, I shared it with my friends. Aware of the situation at home, I knew that continuing with my studies would be financially strenuous. Nonetheless, I was confident that I was going to pass my A level so I promptly began applying for university scholarships. I was not selective, any university offered by the funders I was prepared to accept.

Upon completing our final examinations, Matipa had to leave and pay her brother a visit in Botswana. I was supposed to go home too at once as it had been long since I had last been home but Pablo was hosting a farewell party scheduled within 4 days after my last exam. I had promised not to miss it and adding a few more days to my city stay surely would not hurt anyone. Whenever the squad came together for a good time, we had it.

Pablo arranged a clubhouse for the party. There was alcohol, meat and food. It was a thrilling experience. Just as we were having a whale of a time the guys begun dispersing one after the other to socialise with the surprise guests invited by Pablo. Unwary, I was startled to see Runyararo. I realised she was not alone when I noticed a group of girls whom Pablo had invited to join in the farewell party. Everyone was in a state of euphoria. Awkward as it was, I approached her.

10 The Reveal

I can hardly summon up all the events of that night including how it had ended. I retain being woken up in the morning by Lowe as we needed to tidy up the clubhouse before leaving. High school was a short and significant period of my life, where I learnt, grew and before I realized it, all I had left were memories.

I had been home for almost a fortnight without paying either of my friends a visit nor had they paid me one. I could have assumed that they were not aware of my return but Nyamhere was not that big to not know of one returning home from the city. Thus, we were discernibly avoiding each other. Sad, had our brotherhood come to this? If these were the perks of growing up, then I wished we did not have to grow.

After deciding not to be one who fosters resentment, I took it upon myself to pay Maneta and Chamuka a visit.

"Aah Mukomana," said Maneta walking out of the *tsapi*[52] when he saw me approaching.

---

[52] Granary

He had to bend his head as the door was rather too short for his height. My friend had grown into an audacious and masculine fellow. One would assume he lived to eat only but seeing how jam-packed the granary he was walking out of was, he was evidently doing the hard yards.

Right forearm firm shake followed by a top body hug with the left hand was how we greeted each other. His family followed out of the granary right after him. Wisdom had taken his father's stature, the more he grew the more he looked like the young fellow with whom I had gone herding. He ran towards me, I was not surprised, not that he knew me but he was an easy going and a friendly young champ just like his father. I could not help but lift him up. As if his looks were not enough, when I threw him a little into the air, he even giggled the same way that Maneta used to. I looked at Maneta whilst holding Wisdom, "This one is an imprint of you my friend."

With a chortle Rugare joined into the conversation, "I always tell him, if he had rejected his child, he would have been the clown to the circus for the whole village." At that we shared a moment of laughter, even little Wisdom laughed.

Holding her right elbow with her left hand she extended her right hand towards me, a customary greeting gesture that showed respect. I shook her hand with a smile and handed her the little boy from my arms. She immediately put him down as he was kicking on her grown tummy. Yes, a second imprint was being expected. They were pleasingly growing into a big happy family as I watched.

We conversed for a short while and then she excused herself so as to give my friend and I some space. A slight moment of envy weighed on me as she kissed my friend, took her son and left. Maneta was very fortunate to have the best of both lives, from a fairly fulfilling upbringing to finding love easily. The one girl I had known him to have kept his eyes on he had gotten married to her and he was enjoying having a happy family as well as good yields. I could not help but wonder at the back of my mind if the future held such happiness for me too.

Our catch-up session took longer than expected. When all was said and done it was eventide and I left for home. On the other hand, I could not believe what he had told me. I surely was expecting it but the reality of it cut to a greater depth causing me to feel forlorn. If I could escape it, I would have.

For a while after I got home, I was plagued, until on the second day after my visit to Maneta I decided to ask mama about it.

"Mama, so has Miriro been coming to help you as she usually did?"

"Aah Miriro, which world have you been living in? You have been here for almost a month and you tell me you haven't heard of what happened to Miriro?"

I knew at once that what Maneta had told me was true but I could not make sense of it.

"What happened to her?"

"Your friend, mmh by the way what is his name? This one who likes joking around."

"Mmh Chamuka?"

"*Ehe.*"[53] They got married last year when you did not come for the holidays. As we speak, they have a baby together. I am not sure if it's a girl or a boy."

"Oh, really I didn't know," with a low voice I responded. I had no one to blame for feeling this way. I knew already but I kept on asking for confirmation and in doing so I hit my toe with a hammer. Mama could sense my devastation.

"Don't worry, even I was defeated. I honestly thought Miriro would be my daughter-in-law with all the time she would come to keep me company and assist me. If anything, my heart was hurt more than yours."

As usual mama always responded to my defence; whether she meant to comfort me, which I appreciated, she was venting her truth, it was not helping nor would it change anything.

"No mama I'm not hurt; after all it was not like she was my girlfriend. I'm actually happy for her and you know already I am with Matipa now."

"Matipa was your blessing *mwanangu*[54], and Miriro she would have been a problem. And matter of fact is I'm actually happy for you."

"So, when was the last time you saw her?"

"A week after you left, she came here with her grandmother to introduce me. I even thought it was a gesture of good faith so that we know each other, until when the old lady started coming alone. She was telling me about how she senses spirits over this house claiming how it will take a life what, ahh *mashura*[55]."

---

[53] yes

[54] my child

[55] An abomination

Mama had a point, I remember Miriro had told me that her grandmother was old to be walking around. For her to walk this far from her house it must have been important, but none of us was unwell and as for my parents I would vouch on their behalf they would never do anything with the intention to harm or offend anyone. So why would any spirits haunt them? Since mama seemed unbothered about it, I also decided to overlook it.

Baba had opened a grain mill at the growth point. Whilst I was on holiday, he had delegated me to oversee it. I gladly took on his suggestion as it would keep me occupied whilst awaiting the A Level results which would see to my going to university. As days passed, I enjoyed serving at the mill. I got the opportunity to meet more people who stayed around the village and engage in conversations with them.

One afternoon I was taken by surprise by Miriro's unanticipated visit to the mill. Although I was bound to meet her, our mill was the closest mill at the centre of the five villages. Unlike everyone who would come to the mill she did not have a sack of grains that needed to be grinded. "Surprise, surprise! I was wondering what you guys have been eating. Chamu and you are the only people I've not seen here thus far."

"Is that how educated people greet?"

"Hahahahaha, I'm trying to be welcoming."

"Well, I don't feel welcomed."

"Fair enough, how can I redo my gesture of welcoming you?"

"How about, hello Miriro nice to see you, please here take a seat."

"Okay sorry, hello Miriro nice to see you, please come over and take a seat here."

With a smile she took a seat on the bench I had gestured her towards. "Thank you, that's better," she said as she sat.

Three ladies carrying sacks of mealies on their heads came into the mill, business first so at once I excused myself and went to attend to them. Miriro remained behind sitting as I tended to the customers. I absently poured the mealies from the sacks, emptying them into buckets and from buckets into the grinding machine, putting the empty sacks at the opening of the feeds discharge cylinder. I did all of this wondering what I was going to say to Miriro as her visit was not in the cards and why she had come to see me here and not at home. Within thirty minutes I was done. I neatly tied the sacks and helped each of the ladies put their respective sack on their heads then I returned to Miriro.

"So where did you leave your child?"

"You've been told too many things by people I see."

"Not by people, by mama and does it matter who told me it's not like it's a lie; you have a child don't you?"

"I don't know you to have this tone; maybe I'm not so welcome."

"Am I supposed to apologise for asking the truth?"

"I'm not here to fight Mutsva. I came to check on you as my friend. Heard from a neighbour that it has been a month since you have returned and I knew Chamuka to be your friend as well but both of us hadn't seen you since your return."

"Seems, you've been the one to be told too many things by people. But thank you. I'm alright and as I see looks like you're also in a good space. How is Chamuka?"

"He's alright. Between you and I, he was speaking of coming to see you and invite you to our house."

"That's alright, tell him I said I'm looking forward to the invite."

"I just said between you and I meaning he mustn't know I told you Mutsva."

"Okay."

"I came here to see you so that we could talk. I wanted to find out how you feel about Chamuka and I being married."

"I'm okay with that as long as you are both happy."

"I looked to you as my older brother Mutsva and your mother as my mother. I could never repay you enough for the kindness and care you both showed me. I would be hurt for anything to come between our friendship."

"As I said Miriro, I'm okay with it."

"Mutsva, I know you're just saying it but I can sense the resentment."

"I don't understand how you got to choose my friend but what does it matter?"

"It's clear you are not keen on talking about it but I want you to know that I respect and value our friendship."

"That's alright."

"Another thing before I go. I don't know if I had told you about my grandmother being a *n'anga*[56]."

"No, you just told me she was old."

"Okay, I did not see the need to but she is. I introduced her to your mother in hope for them to become friends but it did not work exactly that way when she told mama what she was sensing; spirits of unrest at your homestead."

"Yes, mama told me."

"Mutsva, I know your family don't believe in it but I

---

[56] Traditional healer

know my grandmother. I've been by her side throughout my life and I affirm you she is an honest traditional healer. What she feels and sees transpires and where she can help, she does with everything she has. She has no ill intentions. I'm concerned about you all and if possible, I wanted to ask if you can come with me to see her so she explains everything to you."

Never had I thought I would dread Miriro's company. If my mother had shown no interest to listening to her grandmother, obviously, I would also share the same sentiment. Our conversation had been unpleasant enough. With a smirk, I brought it to an abrupt end. I stood up. "I hear you, thank you for your concern. I'll think about it." She too stood up and with an implausible smile she said *bye* and left.

Towards the end of January, the 'A' Level results were published. As expected, Uncle Nongai impatiently went to DUB and was informed of my results. He keenly called Baba and shared with him how I had excelled and attained fifteen points. The conversation regarding my tertiary studies with my parents or Uncle Nongai and mainini was still pending. I decided to wait for them to initiate the discussion as I felt awful from the assumption that my studying was becoming a financial burden to them. They did not know of my application for a scholarship.

It had never happened before, being home and having to leave without seeing Chamuka. I left home for Harare with the intention to figure out the way forward regarding my academics then return home to inform my parents. Uncle Nongai came to fetch me from the bus terminus, as before. He was exultant with my academic excellence. To match the energy of excitement, I assumed he would be pleased and proud to know that I intended on furthering my studies.

"I'm impressed and proud of you son but to be honest tertiary education is rather too costly for me at the moment."

I was expecting him to say it as much as I had hoped that he would continue to support me. I understood where he was coming from, nonetheless, his frank disclosure came as an abrupt stumbling block concerning my studies. Dimly, filled with discouragement I responded, "I hear you babamunini. It's okay. We will have to see the way forward."

Uncle Nongai was in a better financial space than my father. Baba made enough to sustain us as a family, his savings could barely pay for an annual period of tertiary studies. The only remaining chance that stood for me was the presidential scholarship. I had not shared anything with anyone with regards to it lest I gave them false hope. I myself was not sure if I stood the chance to get it as the student-pool of demand was over crowded. Our discussion made the rest of the journey home tense. I did not know what to say lest I lied about how I was feeling or hurt his feelings.

When we got home, we found Meme and Mimi impatiently waiting at the gate. We had most certainly missed each other. As I got off the car, they both ran towards me, such a warm welcome full of love and good cheer, I excitedly bent to their height and hugged them both at once.

11 A Whirlwind

In the middle of the night my body felt heavy. I struggled to wake up. I needed a toilet break. After using all the strength, I suppose I had, I managed to put one foot off the bed on to the ground for balance then I eventually managed. When I woke up in the morning, I recalled how I had struggled to wake up during the night and there was nothing to dismiss that I actually had encountered sleep paralysis. It was during the second term; schools were open therefore it was only Sisi and I left in the house during the day. After an ineffective follow up with the presidential scholarship, it was certain that 1999 would be a repeat of 1991, my dreams and aspirations put on halt. I despised being a victim of circumstances and yet life had its own way of always finding a way to drive me into such a situation.

The sleep paralysis continued for three more days and I could not bring myself to understanding what was happening to me or my body because it persisted even during the day. I would frequently find myself falling asleep during the day probably out of boredom. I then decided to weed around the yard that way I would keep myself busy and avoid sleeping during the day.

It being a very sunny and hot day, within thirty minutes of my attempt I began feeling drained as if I was going to faint, so I gave up and at once I returned to my bedroom.

"Knock Mutsva," said mainini Maggie as she asked for an invitation to get into my room.

"Come in," I responded and remained lying down because I felt too weak to sit up.

"We need to talk my child," she said claiming a sit on the corner of my bed where she could see my face. "I'm worried about you. Sisi tells me you sleep till midday and when you wake up you barely eat and you return to sleep once again and in the evenings we barely see you."

I could not tell her of what I was feeling as there could not have been any words to best describe it. "You don't have to worry mainini. I'm fine thank you. I'll work on it so you don't have to worry."

"Okay if you say so. If you need to talk let me know. This idea of taking a gap year could be weighing heavy on you, I'm aware but don't allow it to take a toll on you; it's just for a year as we save up for your study tuition."

"Mainini I'm okay," I said with a dismissive grin.

She was probably coming at me from a good place out of concern but she had absolutely the wrong idea of what was going on with me. She smiled back and left the room not completely shutting the door. Uncle Nongai was standing just outside my bedroom door. It was clearly a pre-discussed conversation and I could hear them mutter as they walked away. Their conversation became inaudible in no time but from what I had heard, they were diagnosing me with depression.

I was disappointed and demotivated by the thought of not being able to further my studies that year as I had expected and prepared myself to do but me having depression was an overstatement. Against my body's will I began waking up early and would find ways to keep myself occupied during the day to avoid sleeping. Despite not having appetite, I shoved food down my throat, which would occasionally make me nauseas but I would manage to keep it in. It took more energy for me to go on about my day. When I would retire to bed my relief was significant. I sighed as if I had gone through a long day of manual labour.

For a week it continued, however it became clear that I was not at my best self no matter how much I had tried to cover up and commit to my daily routines. One morning I was up and vomiting. As weak as my body felt, I had at least 3 trips to the bathroom. I threw up everything I had eaten till I was empty of anything to throw up. Mainini took my temperature; I was hypothermic and I was shivering too.

When we got to Parirenyatwa Hospital I was admitted. Two days after running tests on me the root cause was unfound. The nausea and vomiting stopped but my temperature began going abnormally high. Based on the pyrexia I was having, the Doctor put me on antibiotics and pain medication to alleviate the fever. It did help reduce the temperature but I still shivered. I was discharged and given treatment to continue taking.

Being sick as a visitor I figured overburdened Uncle Nongai and mainini; I had to go back home. My condition would not have been conducive for me to job hunt during my gap year, so I asked to go back home. Aunty Maggie insisted that Uncle Nongai had to drive me home. He drove whilst I slept through the whole journey.

On arriving home mama who had been informed of my illness came to greet us in great despair, gravely wailing on top of her voice. If being sick caused such great distraught to my mother, God forbid ***but*** my death surely would be hers too. I was the ill one but I had to hold her in support from falling and rolling on the ground and we went into the house. Uncle Nongai did not stay long. Immediately after seeing mama and baba and carrying my luggage into the living room, he left instructing me to finish my course of medication.

The idea was to be home, in my comfortable space so I would heal quicker but it felt as if it was just the beginning. Adding onto the body weakness, I began passing diarrhoea and the vomiting got worse that I would vomit blood. On one afternoon, I passed out for the longest time. When I woke up mama was overjoyed with tears streaming down her face and at once baba also walked in with the pastor whom they had called to pray for me. I had suffered a seizure, which they had presumed had taken my life. After the prayer, mama served supper. Due to my illness, I had severely refrained from eating. When the pastor left, baba accompanied him out. If anything, I wanted to get well for mama. She was wasting away.

Being at home reminded me of the things said by Miriro's grandmother about 'a spirit over this house claiming it will take a life'. Could we have ignored a significant message? The thought of my life being on the verge of being taken away troubled and scared me that I got the courage to ask my mother. "Do you ever wonder if what is happening to me is what Miriro's grandmother was trying to warn us about?"

"No, are you mad?"

"Mama you're the one who told me that she mentioned to you something about a spirit over this house claiming it will take a life."

"If there were a spirit over this house that wanted to take anyone's life, do you think any of us would have lived to this day? Such a spirit can only belong to the devil. The Bible mentions the Devil's passion is to steal, kill and destroy. And to attain that he does so impatiently. You think he would've waited for an old lady to see his intentions before striking? All of a sudden there is a spirit? Yes of course, the Holy Spirit of God and he watches over us fear not my child, he will heal you."

She was enraged. I did not wish to exacerbate her state so I let the conversation die away by not asking any further questions with regards to that subject.

My illness was not resolving despite the numerous visits that I had done to the village clinic. In an attempt to get a second opinion baba had even taken me to the general hospital of Mutare. I kept on taking the prescribed, however ineffective medication. I had lost me in the past weeks. The illness that weighed heavy on my body was not resolving. I was tired. All the possible energy in me had withered away together with my hope, dreams and desires. All had been tried but unfortunately to no avail. I just wanted all the pain, the heaviness of my body, the periodical vomiting and diarrhoea episodes to stop. I yearned for a chance to rest.

Mama could see how dispirited I was, I noticed how she barely left my side and when she would leave, she would try to engage me in a conversation no matter how far apart we were, just to keep me from slipping into sleep.

Melodiously, singing to a church hymn mama sat at the entrance of my bedroom door weaving her reeds mat. A visitor's knock drew her attention. As she went to attend to the knock, I was relieved to have her preoccupied. I just needed a little silence to relax.

After being drawn into another long deep sleep I was woken up by sprinkles of water on my face. My room was covered in what seemed like smoke or mist. From outside through my window, I could hear my mother wailing at the top of her voice "*amai kani iii amai kani iii*"[57]. It seemed she was wrestling another woman who was trying to hold her still. Before I could make sense of what was happening the smoke was choking me. I had no energy to cough. On attempt to cough I seemingly took a gasp of it and intoxicated I fell asleep again.

A lot had happened by the time I woke up again. My head was resting on mama's lap and baba was sitting on a stool besides mama. Miriro sat by the entrance where mama sat earlier on and she was holding her child in her arms. I was awakened by what my eyes caught in the far end corner. Someone unidentifiable, covered and overwhelmingly dressed in what looked like a brown blanket but it also appeared to have a baggy fur of a bear and she wore hair made up of beads which continuously shook as she swayed her head round and round. The exposed bare feet showed that she was a female. She sat on the floor with her legs open at a sixty-degree angle. In-between her legs on the ground lay what looked like stones of different shapes. She begun hoarsely burping, very loud and with every burp she would move her body back and forth.

Miriro then instructed my parents to clap along with her; they all began clapping. I was not dreaming nor did I

---

[57] Mother, mother! (cry of agony)

understand what was happening but I assumed Miriro's grandmother to have been the one sitting in the far end corner. The joint thudding of their claps continued until she lifted up her white staff which looked as if it were made of horse tail and she pointed it at me.

"Uyu! iwewe, iyewe,[58]" she called out pointing her stuff towards me still with her head facing down. I had no idea how to respond to her. I probably would have said yes? Neither mama nor baba also knew how to respond so they both looked at Miriro to advise on what to say or do next.

---

[58] this one! you, yes you

12 Unconcealed Truth

'*Malo nodo malus quaerendus cuneus.*[59]' Erasmus's Latin proverb was the only way to explain how mama had been convinced to let Miriro's grandmother attend to my illness by means of her special gift. It had been an appalling past few weeks for my family and I, as I had faded and remarkably lost weight. None of us knew what exactly had made me so unwell as my illness was medically assessed to no avail of a conclusive diagnosis, but that was no longer of our concern as my wellbeing had been refurbished.

It was then when my family and I learned that Gogo Mudanda was an esteemed traditional healer bestowed with special spiritual gifts to be a seer and healer. My family had not been the one to invest in understanding of such practices. However, at that moment we hardly had a choice except to pay attention to the remedy that she had used to heal me.

---

[59] Desperate times call for desperate measures!

"*Hatisati Tapedza,*"[60] meaning we are not done as yet, was Gogo Mudanda's statement when she left. Adding to my confusion was how after a couple of hours with a rush of dark smoke filling up my bedroom, Gogo Mudanda groaning and roaring it seemed as if I was wearing a new body. Unable to comprehend what had transpired I just sat on top of my blankets awaiting to hear what mama or baba had to say. They both sat motionless, I assumed they would know better the right words to utter in such an unusual situation. The silence that filled the room was evident that baba and mama shared the same sentiment with me. None of us understood what was happening and we were all in bewilderment of what we had seen.

"Let me go to the kitchen and figure out what to cook," said mama as she dismissed herself fleeing to the kitchen. I wanted to understand what was happening or what had happened.

"I am feeling way much better. I can't believe I was fatally ill for all this time to only be better after being done things in an hour."

"Mutsva even I too don't know," he said shaking his head with wonder. "I just realised we do not know it all. I saw things I have never seen being done by a person before and heard voices and sounds I have never heard. I am just relieved that all of this was not done for nothing my child."

After a while, mama broke the silence that baba and I were sharing as she walked in with a dish and water for washing hands and she knelt to let Baba wash his hands.

[60] We are not yet done

"So, is it possible and acceptable to say this is a miracle or are miracles only referred to in the Christian doctrine?"

"Mmh what else can this be besides a miracle," said mama as she came to give me the dish and let me wash my hands too. "From what I have witnessed here, I believe good deeds be it behind the Holy Spirit or the ancestral spirit, they work hand in hand. They seem to be inclusive rather than competitive because at the end of the day the main focus is to attain healing and purity." Mama stood up and left for the kitchen to get the food, leaving baba and I deep in wonder.

What Gogo Mudanda meant about not being done was that she had instructed us to meet her at Mushamhuru, where mama had found me twenty years earlier. Seemingly, I figured out what she intended to address. As much as I had no desire to reconnect with my background we also knew better; it was important to take heed of what she would say. After a week Miriro paid us a visit and she informed us that Gogo had found the medication she needed and was ready to meet us and finish up.

The following morning at dawn, mama and I went to meet Gogo Mudanda at the stream. She reminded mama of where exactly she had found me. After that she asked us to follow her to an unnamed place. She sang all the way. Mama and I obediently followed without uttering anything. By midmorning I was tired of walking. We passed through Muromo bottle store. At the fifth homestead after the bottle store, she stopped and called us to come and stand with her. She held my hand, smiled and said,

"I want you to know this. You don't choose where you come from, where you come from chooses you and you are chosen for a reason".

She let go off my hand and started clapping as she entered the yard. Without saying anything mama and I followed her, we were received by an elderly gentleman who gave us a place to seat and he introduced his wife to us as she joined. After exchanging greetings, she offered us something to eat or drink but Gogo refused, which compelled us to do likewise. Gogo started crying. None of us were ready for that. Mama and I just looked at each other puzzled and helpless; the gentleman's wife reached out to console her. She continued sobbing then after she was calm, she thanked her and asked her to revert to her seat.

"Is this Vimbai's home?" asked Gogo.

"It is yes; she is our daughter but she doesn't stay here, she stays at her matrimonial home," kindly and warmly she responded. And with reassurance she continued, "It's not far, if need be, we could ask someone to go and call her for you or we could go to her house."

Gogo asked for Vimbai to come as this issue needed to be addressed not in her matrimonial home. Vimbai was sent for and within half an hour two ladies walked in and greeted us. They claimed their seats on the reeds mat that had been put on the floor. Of the two ladies, the older one upon exchanging greetings addressed the gentleman who had received us as 'Shewe[61]' and he had responded by calling her *ahanzvadzi,* meaning sister.

"Vimbai the visitors you see here came looking for you and they asked us to call for you. This is Vimbai and with her is her father's sister," said Vimbai's mother introducing us.

---

[61] a name given out of respect to a man

"I was actually on my way to come and pay you a visit and I thought to pass by Vimbai's house and see how she is doing. The word came that she was being called for at home just as I was about to leave," Shewe's sister responded eager to hear what Vimbai had been called for.

"So, we came together."

"Vimbai, where is Panganai," asked Gogo.

Startled she jumped to respond with a defensive tone, "I have no idea; it's been twenty or more years since he was last seen in this village. Ever since he decided to go and join the freedom fighters".

"You made us seat like this, all of us to talk about that? I think you need to learn to respect people's time," responded Shewe as he stood wearing great fury.

His wife reached for his hand and asked him to take his seat. Politely he returned to his seat.

Gogo continued, "You see this young man with me is Panganai's son and he is twenty years old and the lady sitting next to him is his mother but not by birth. In as much as you concealed it, Panganai knows about his son and he is with immense rage of being denied the chance of connecting with him. He wants his son to know about him and his family. Vimbai, the spirit has brought me here as you gave birth to this young man. You may know better how we can get to his family?"

As Gogo spoke, Vimbai's mother looked at me with a piercing stare. I tried avoiding looking back at her but I could not. I caught sight of her eyes; they were drained in tears. Vimbai shared the same look as her father, irritated, angry and annoyed. Suddenly, he stood in haste and left without uttering a word. We shared a while of a lull before the storm.

Vimbai was not pleased to learn about me, "And who are you," she asked looking at Gogo.

"That is not important. Take us to Panganai's home," responded Gogo in disbelief of Vimbai's reaction and response.

"I have nothing against this boy. But it wasn't my fault that his father disappeared on me and left me out of solutions. At least he got a good mother."

"Vimbai," called Shewe's sister, authoritatively calling her to order.

"Sure Tete Vee. I don't want to have anything implicating my marriage and my family," Vimbai callously responded.

"We're not asking you to take him in to your house. He is my son and he has a family which is happy to have him. Just take us to Panganai's home and spare us all this drama," responded mama.

In disbelief, I kept quiet, listening to the back and forth of the conversations. I was stunned, to think Vimbai was the woman who gave birth to me. Her resentment released me from being entrapped in wonder of my origins. I just wanted to get it all over and done with and return home. All this was not important to me. However, it seemed imperative to get to know Panganai and his family. Shewe' s sister eventually managed to convince Vimbai to take us to Panganai's family as unwilling as she seemed.

A young lady welcomed us as we entered the yard Vimbai was leading us in to. She spread out a reeds mat under the shade of the huge fig tree and allowed us to sit as she went to call the elders. The tension between mama and Vimbai did not make it any easy. The six of us, mama, Gogo Mudanda, Vimbai, her mother, her father's sister and I, sat mutely and expectantly waiting. Two old gentlemen walked out of the house followed by an elderly, short and fair skinned lady. The young lady at once returned with two wooden stools and placed them at a small distance from us. We exchanged greetings and the two gentlemen sat down.

The elderly lady greeted me last and as she did, she grasped on to my hand and she looked at me with wonder. She raised her hands reaching for my face. Her rough palms touching my face startled me but I did not want to be rude and remove her hands off my face. She started with laughing then at once tears began falling on her face flowing over the smile lines at the corners of her mouth.

She muttered how much I was an embodiment of her son. The sight of me made her relive the grief of losing him. Panganai had unfortunately never returned home; they knew not of his whereabouts. She narrated the last time they saw him and it matched the days I was conceived. Gogo Mudanda had taken us on a hunt for a probably deceased man. What did I need to know about a dead man? I thought to myself whilst sitting exhausted.

It was just after dusk, Panganai's mother insisted on us staying for the night because she wanted to make a special meal to honour my visit. Gogo agreed, which saw mama and I doing the same but Vimbai and her mother together with Shewe's sister turned down the offer and returned to their house. Before leaving, Vimbai whispered to mama's ear. She could have possibly asked mama to never bring me back in to her life, not that I was bothered by it at all.

After the evening meal, the young lady who had ushered us on arrival cleaned up the kitchen and prepared a place for us to sleep. At the crack of dawn, I woke up ready to journey back home. On the face of it, I was not the only one looking forward to leaving, I was the last one to wake up. Through the stripes of the wooden door, I could see a giant flame that was outside. *Could they have woken up earlier to extinguish the fire?* At that thought in haste I woke up, ran out with the intention to assist lest we be blamed for bringing with us the bad luck.

I was confronted by a structured built ring of fire. On one side mama and Panganai's mother together with the two older men sat on the ground and on the far end. Gogo Mudanda sat covered in her brown blanket with the baggy fur of a bear and she wore on her head a hairpiece made up of beads, she continuously shook her head to all sides, hoarsely burping, very loud and with every burp she would move her body back and forth just as she had previously done in my room.

Mama saw me and with her hand she instructed me to come and sit with her. As I sat Gogo began speaking in a deep hoarse voice, the base was that of a man. Mama must have remembered how previously Miriro had asked us to clap; she started clapping and I did likewise, followed by everyone else sitting around the fire.

"*Amai,* my son will continue from where I left!" said Gogo Mudanda in the weird voice.

Clapping her hands, Panganai's mother responded to Gogo yet looking at me. She asked me if I was willing to accept the gift which my supposed father was handing over to me. The gift of being a *n'anga, which means traditional healer.* Apparently, she was also a *n'anga*, and a seer. The tradition followed passing of this gift on to your first offspring. As Panganai had received it from his mother, he wanted me to be aware of it as it had to be passed on to me. Accepting it meant that I was acknowledging and accepting the gift of being a traditional healer and a seer. There was no room for denial, at that point the sequence of events seemed as if I was already being instigated to becoming one. Choiceless, I nodded my head in acceptance and she stood up, ululating and dancing as she stomped her feet on the dusty ground.

After the moment of celebration Gogo Mudanda asked for attention, she had resumed to her usual way of speaking. "This is a special gift Mutsva. I know it's not easy. It may come with challenges but you will learn ways that will see you through. We're all happy and we celebrate thanking you for accepting this gift passed on to you by your father. He may now be at rest as you take over the purpose."

"*Sure iyoyo*[62]," Panganai's mother answered in approval.

The other gentlemen uttered to each other, their indistinct conversations beyond the reach of my ears did not seem as if they were in disagreement with what we were all hearing.

She continued putting emphasize to what Gogo Mudanda had said, "Your first house and first family to accept you were the reeds in which you were left in following your birth. Nature took on the responsibility that was unexpectedly given to it, made a home for you and watched over you. The reeds did justice to you more than the supposed bond of the blood between you and Vimbai."

One of the elderly gentlemen stood and spoke in agreement, "*Wagona watenda chipo chako mukomana*[63], you were watched over to fulfil a purpose such as this."

No one knew where Panganai had been buried as he had given himself into the liberation struggle. What we

---

[62] That's true

[63] well done for accepting your gift

knew was my acceptance of the gift he was passing on to me was going to make his spirit and soul be at rest. Panganai had passed on the relay stick of responsibilities to me and I had accepted to continue and embrace the gift which Gogo Mudanda had mentioned to be 'a gift for the people'.

No wonder why the forest had been my sanctuary, Panganai's spirit had been hovering over it and watching over me for this intended purpose. This explained my understanding of herbal and plant remedies. I did not share this realization with mama but I knew accepting the gift of being a healer and a seer meant that I could no longer ignore my natural skill on the use of herbal remedies, I had to embrace who I was.

13 Embracing it all

When we left Panganai's home, his mother had unfortunately been unable to finish teaching me on how to go about practicing the use of the gift and skill so she offered to be my mentor. Mama and I accepted the offer as we knew no one else who would be in a better position to teach me.

When we shared with Baba our experience, he expressed how relieved he was that I had received help and the disappointment which we all shared towards how Vimbai had received the news about me.

Mama and Panganai's mother grew close as she would often pay us a visit where she would in turn take me on educative escapades. We grew to understand each other and learnt the different ways of life we lived, which we managed to incorporate and learn from each other. My gap year highlight was all the knowledge I attained of being a traditional healer. Being equipped with both the skill and ability to attend to illnesses traditionally and using western methods acquired from the medical school would be my greatest life accomplishment. As I awaited with a ray of hope for a scholarship and an opportunity to further my studies, I continued enriching my knowledge base on becoming a better and skilled traditional healer.

Each day I discovered something interestingly new. With respect to herbal treatment, natural medicine as Gogo Mudanda preferred it to be called, the more knowledge I acquired on it the more curious I grew and my potent smell instinct came as an extra aid in carrying out the assignments given to me by Gogo.

One afternoon, I returned home from my sprees and found Gogo Mudanda sitting with my mom under the mango tree. They seemed to be having a merry chat. Who would have thought that my mother and Miriro's grandmother would ever get along? I suppose I could take the credit, my near-death illness contributed to their compassionate reconciliation and knowing mama she probably felt she owed her for saving my life. I held no grudge with Gogo Mudanda. It pleased me to see her and mama getting along but I was not yet ready to do likewise with Miriro and Chamu. The pain I felt from their unintended betrayal lingered like a dark fog in my mind and heart. I owed no one for saving my life, I had saved Miriro's life too; if anything, we were square.

After greeting the two ladies, I was confronted by Gogo Mudanda with an interrogation of what I was holding. After explaining to her the names and use of each of the four different stalks I held, she nodded in satisfaction and smiled at the realisation that she did not do all she did for me in vain. Mama and Baba shared the same sentiment, I had learnt the proceedings of being a traditional healer at a very quick pace.

Next to her was the sack of mealies, she had brought but had unfortunately found the grain mill closed. I still honoured my task of overseeing the grain mill. However, on other days I would close early so as to attend to other duties hence she had missed me. Out of courtesy I offered to take it with me the following morning. Rest assured mama had already made that suggestion to her new friend in my absentia. I left them to continue before being drawn into their conversations.

The following day was Sunday, my parents and I woke up to prepare for church. Yes, I did go to church too! I had a gift, an ability to know the use of some products of nature with regard to treating illness, generationally conceded. I believed in God being the creator of the universe, nature was according to his design. Certainly, he intended for it to be used for healing purposes. However, my attendance at church was questioned by a number of individuals who held leadership positions in the church. One of the elders confronted my father concerning how acceptance of my gift and manner of practice was not in alignment with the Christian way of life. My life had ways of constantly getting into a vicious cycle of Catch-22 situations. I was in a predicament as I could not choose between my gift or my Christian values as both of them were my source of identity. They were both of great value to me. Why could I not live with both? It is the question I had persistently asked mama and my father with great concern until they resolved that we would begin attending church as a family at home going forward.

Everyone in the village who came to my grain mill knew that it would be closed on Sunday's. Therefore, I assumed Gogo Mudanda would not expect her mealie meal until Monday. Usually, after church my family and I spent the rest of the day, relaxing and sharing time together. I would discuss about the mill and gave baba all the profits of the week. After, it would be time for an afternoon nap, which would see me heading for my room, leaving mama and baba in the sitting room.

On that particular Sunday baba asked me not to leave. He instead left for his bedroom, leaving mama and I in the sitting room curiously waiting for his return. As he walked back, our eyes accompanied him as he took his seat with wonder of what was in the box that he was carrying.

"Nongai called me on Friday. He gave me a number. I wrote it down on a piece of paper," said baba as he reached for his pocket. With a smile he continued, "Right, here it is. Apparently, the call was for you Mutsva; I see people are calling everywhere and everyone looking for you so I saw it fit to get you your own phone. It will also help you with managing the grain mill, especially with people starting to look for you."

With my eyes opened in disbelief with a huge smile. I motionlessly starred at baba as it was just as unexpected as it was a pleasant gift.

"*Tora ka Mutsva, gamuchira po tione,*[64]" said mama impatiently as she was just as eager to see as I was.

"Thank you," I said clapping my hands as baba handed to me the phone.

Before I could handover to mama the gift baba had given me, I had to wait until she was done with her prance and ululation.

"This is nice. Go on and open the box; also get the number from Baba, let us call and hear who is looking for

---

64 Take Mutsva, receive and let us see

you *mwanangu* hehehe. When it rings ngri nori ngri nori *wochodai*[65] Hello, hello," said mama putting the phone on her ear.

I had to charge the battery and put in a net one line for me to be able to make a call but mama would not know nor understand about all of that so I let her continue with her ecstatic amusement.

The following morning, the first thing I did on getting to the mill was put my phone on the charger, grinded Miriro's grandmother's grain and placed it where I would not forget to carry it home with me. I was excited to learn of who had been looking for me, I was hoping it would be Matipa. Unfortunately, it had not been her nor was it anyone I knew off. The recipient of my call spoke formally to me. He asked for my biography and he confirmed the information against the data he had and promised to get back at me. I dismissed all the excitement I had and knew better than to raise my hopes and expectations. I was not that important for someone to call me back. He was never going to call me back. I proceeded to clean up my workspace and as soon as I was done, a queue of clients waiting with their sacks of grain awaited me.

After tending to my customers without a break, it was nightfall and I was exhausted. On locking up, I remembered I had a phone. As I went to collect it, I had the door of the mill opening and yet I had closed it. Quickly, I disconnected my phone, leaving the charger on the socket so I could get to see who had opened the door. Before I could see I heard who it was. Instantly, I felt my blood boiling. The disrespect that Chamu had, the nerve to invade my space uninvited. Maneta being there with

---

[65]You do this

him barely helped with keeping me calm. I did not want to see him. I could not figure out why he was trying to provoke me. I walked to find them giggling standing by the door. Seeing Gogo Mudanda's sack of grinded mealie meal which I had left besides the door drew me into reserving my actions. Perhaps he had come out of call of duty.

"Maneta, Chamuka," I greeted them, initiating the conversation and stood right in front of them. If they had not been in the doorway, I would have stood outside, ready to leave and lock up.

"*Wangu-u-u,*[66]" said Chamuka as he excitedly stretched his hands to greet me. For one who once resented Maneta for marrying his sister, I expected him to know better and understand how I felt. In haste I picked the sack of mealie meal and handed it to his outstretched hand.

"I think you are here for this."

Maneta silently observed, as he was rightfully expected to because when they had their strife, I had not interfered nor chosen sides.

"Thank you, yes! Gogo sent me. I was actually glad she sent me here. It forced me to put all my errands on hold and make way to come and also see you my friend."

The nerve he had to continue as if everything between us was alright. I could not believe how thoughtless Chamuka was. In disgust and out of words for him I just stood looking at him. I wanted to push him out and Maneta would freely follow his companion that way I could lock my door and leave the selfish fool.

---

[66] mine

"I see it's already clean and the mill is off. Are you done for the day already?" asked Maneta trying to alleviate the tension in the room.

I responded to him by swinging the keys I held on my right and he nodded in approval. Gently, he walked out the door. Chamuka obediently picked up Gogo Mudanda's parcel in his right hand and went ahead to load it onto his cart and they both climbed into the cart ready to go. After locking my door, I waived to them and headed for home. As much as it was late and dark, I felt safer walking home than taking cover by riding in the backstabber's cart. After all, nature and I were merged from birth, it was my first home and provision of safety.

Chamuka's arrogance and ignorance annoyed me. He did not see any wrong in what he had done. Convinced, I thought to myself how we were never going to be able to resolve the dilemma because of his attitude. However, Maneta driven by the pledge of undying brotherhood took it upon himself and made a mission to catalyse my reconciliation with Chamuka. Following weeks of nagging me to engage in a conversation with Chamuka, I gave in to his persuasion and agreed to meet with both of them and address the issue together. Maneta being there would help me keep my calm because the sight alone of Chamuka infuriated me.

Late afternoon, I sat under the fig tree enjoying the shade and cool breeze it gave. How such a huge tree would grow on a rocky surface and also have its giant roots spread over the rock really amazed me. On such days, when the mill was not busy, I would delight myself to the sight of the activities around the growth point. I would sit and watch people walking in and out of different stores. The interesting havoc at the corner where a group of gentlemen played chess and the overall best was watching the drama that transpired at the bottle stores, interactions between the drunk and sober, especially seeing the drunk ladies dance, sing loudly and some dragging each other out of the bottle store with the intention to return home.

When my phone rang, I knew it would be Baba checking up on me and trying to make me get used to the idea of having a mobile phone. My phone rang and I did not recognise the number that showed, I knew it was not baba so I answered with great curiosity. I could not believe the news I had just received; the call had been disengaged. However, I kept starring at my phone in amazement. At once, I wanted to share the incredible news I had received with my parents. The thought of making use of my phone to call Baba and Uncle No and inform them skipped my mind. As I stood up to go home, the noise of cowbells behind my back drew my attention. It was from Chamuka's cow drawn cart which was approaching the mill. They were in it together with Maneta. As busy as Maneta was, for him to make time to come and pay me a visit with Chamuka was a great sacrifice and I respected and appreciated his comradeship.

"A great time to have good company," I said shouting out to them as they climbed off the cart, trying at my utmost polite, calm and welcoming tone because Chamuka was not the kind of company I needed as much as I was happy to see their reconnection.

"Are you not supposed to be in your office busy working, Mr White stuff," responded Maneta as he walked towards my right and claimed a seat for himself on the rocky ground.

"Of course. I decided to leave people to do it for themselves. They should be able to get it right, *hanti ndivo vachadya,*[67]" I said in response to match Maneta's sarcastic question.

Chamuka and I shook hands and he claimed a seat for himself too on my left. I had no choice except to revert to sitting as they clearly were making themselves comfortable with no intention of just passing by.

"Iye Maneta arikubvunza vamwe iye nhasi aripano

chisi here[68]? He never comes out of the field unless it is on the day forbidden by the headman," commented Chamuka trying to warm his way into the conversation, which worked as we all laughed.

"*Mutsva, ndauya naChamuka tigadzirise daka renyu*[69]. We can't continue going on like there is no tension or unaddressed issue."

Why Maneta was putting me or both of us in an awkward space, I have no idea, because I had respected their misunderstanding and allowed them to address it at their own time and own way. This was not the conversation I wanted to engage in at that moment but it needed to be had. Wasting no time, I frankly responded,

"Chamuka after how you responded to the realisation of Maneta marrying your sister, I expected better from you but you did exactly what you disputed; so, did you just expect me to get over it?"

"True I hear you, sure. *Panoda kugadziriswa* [70]the tension between Maneta and I was straining our friendship and

[67] isn't it them who will need to eat?

[68] Maneta himself, he is interrogating you and yet he is here, it's not even a declared sacred day to toil today

[69] Mutsva, I have brought Chamuka so we may resolve the conflict between the two of you

[70] It needs to be solved

Miriro was the one who actually told me about how stressful it was on you to the point of dreading to come back home for your holidays. In order to help restore our brotherhood and make you happy she advised me to make peace with Maneta."

"Oh, so she convinced you?"

"It was a bet. I met her at your house when I paid mama a visit and began seeing her around and at the growth point numerous times but she wouldn't speak to me. She insisted on shunning me with silent treatment and ordered that unless I fixed things with Maneta she would never talk to me".

"Unbelievable! What! Why was it so important for her to have you and Maneta get along?"

"You," he said shaking his head looking at Maneta and I because he knew we could see through him; his charm would not work on us.

Maneta and I both starred at Chamuka. In my mind I screamed, *Liar!* He was basically making up a story to make sure we reconcile. We just wanted him to take responsibility.

"I'm not lying; I know you think I'm making all of this up but she really wanted you to take pleasure in coming home for the holidays as our tension was apparently making you resent returning home."

We both laughed at him, he did not intend to apologise the same way he expected Maneta to apologise.

"Aah guys?"

"We are not laughing at you. It's your story, it doesn't make sense as much as you are trying to convince us."

"*NaMwari O*,[71] it's the truth and she mentioned that Mutsva you were like a brother to her and she felt that you were entrapped and that your life was under threat and apparently the only way to be set free was by you returning home. I know this doesn't make sense, it didn't make sense to me too; but I care about you, probably the same way she cares about you, as a brother. So, to save your life I'd do anything." sincerely continued Chamuka.

Maneta and I we were worn out with laughter because as much as he did not realise it, he was speaking nonsense and him trying to convince us was not making his story credible. Sharing such a moment made me realise that despite what had happened I just wanted our trio-brotherhood back. But Chamuka had to say sorry not this no sense pity story.

"Alright, let's consider you are actually telling the truth..." I failed to finish my sentence as I got caught up with Maneta's laughter he was even lying down on the rock. I managed to recollect myself then I continued, "...Miriro told you, that I was like a brother to her but still *wakapamha iwewe zvakaita Maneta uyu*[72]."

Still laughing Maneta rose to sit up and he reached for Chamuka's shoulders, "*Tsano imimi neni takafanana*[73], what I did is exactly what you did."

"*Nxa haihwawho ibva*,"[74] said Chamuka rubbing Maneta's hand off his shoulder.

---

[71] On God

[72] You repeated what Maneta did

[73] Brother you and I are the same

[74] Get off!

"Ehe chokwadi chinorwadza ka,[75] let me help you and remind you what you made me say to you. You will repeat exactly after me, ok? Sorry I disrespected you and walked into your garden without your permission I plucked off a flower for myself."

Maneta was having the last of the joke to himself I could not help but join him as we made Chamuka have a taste of his own medicine.

"*Nxa.*[76]When you laugh you make it seem as if I'm wrong but I am telling the truth but okay Sorry Mutsva."

From what Chamuka had said Miriro knew about my gift. She knew about the threat to my life. *Could she and I have the same gifts?* Immediately I rubbed the thought off my mind I did not want to have any more unanswered questions weighing on me after I had just gotten the questions that had been lingering in my head all my life just answered.

"It's okay *wangu*," I responded as I reached for Chamuka's back and gave him a pat. "I was just about to leave for home, will you please give me your ride in your cart *Tsano*[77] *kkkkk*, *iwe*[78] Maneta stand up let us go.

His defensive tone showed how much he had rehearsed for the conversation. Fair enough, there was no reason for me to continue being angry at him. Miriro was neither my sister nor my girlfriend as I had never let known my feelings towards her. I had received an offer to commence my studies in Cuba at Universidad de Los Andes in the Faculty of Health Sciences. I had no need to

---

[75] Yes, the truths hurts doesn't it

[76] Sound you make to show you are irritated about something

[77] Brother-in-law

[78] hey

pursue a purposeless resentment. My life was taking a turn for the better, I had grown to know my roots better and got to understand the gift I contained.

In addition to my generic gift, an alternative and academic input to health care would equip me and put me in an exceptional position to care for the wellbeing of folks. I was filled with contentment at the realisation that I had realised my purpose and the events of my life were heading towards full attainment and achievement of it.

As Gogo had mentioned in my dream after her passing, I was advancing towards doing what I was called to do.

THE END

www.ingramcontent.com/pod-product-compliance
Ingram Content Group UK Ltd.
Pitfield, Milton Keynes, MK11 3LW, UK
UKHW020415250726
13967UKWH00007B/2656